#2
BUYING TIME

Stephanie Doyon

Aladdin Paperbacks

First Aladdin Paperbacks edition June 1999

Text copyright © 1999 by Stephanie Doyon

Aladdin Paperbacks
An imprint of Simon & Schuster
Children's Publishing Division
1230 Avenue of the Americas
New York, NY 10020

Designed by Steven M. Scott
The text for this book was set in Wilke Roman.
Printed and bound in the United States of America
10 9 8 7 6 5 4 3 2 1

Library of Congress Cataloging-in-Publication Data
Doyon, Stephanie.
Buying time / by Stephanie Doyon. — 1st Aladdin Paperbacks ed.
p.   cm. — (On the road. Exit ; #2)
Sequel to: Leaving home.
Summary: Just graduated from high school and in the midst of deciding her future, eighteen-year-old Miranda joins her older brother in Virginia, where he is doing volunteer work building houses for the disadvantaged.
ISBN 0-689-82108-5 (pbk.)
[1. Brothers and sisters—Fiction. 2. House construction—Fiction. 3. Voluntarism—Fiction. 4. Virginia—Fiction.]
I. Title. II. Series: Doyon, Stephanie. On the road. Exit ; #2.
PZ7.D7783Bu   1998
[Fic]—dc21   98-52155
CIP   AC

For my nieces—
Serena and Nerissa

Sitting on the wooden bench directly across from me at the Charlottesville bus station are two teenagers with their arms wrapped around each other like they have only one minute left to live. It's sweet—in a really pathetic sort of way. Loverboy is slumped over his girlfriend, practically smothering her with the hollow of his neck. It's a wonder she can get any air in there. They both have their eyes closed (which is why I haven't been busted for staring), and their lips are all pouty and sad. My guess is they're going their separate ways for the summer. I'm sure it feels like the end of the world to them now, but give it a few weeks. Before you know it, he's going to be smothering some other girl and she's going to be having a summer fling with the beach boy of her dreams. By the time fall rolls around, they won't even remember each other's names.

Hey, I'm not saying true love doesn't happen. I'm just saying it doesn't happen as often as most people want to believe. *Like* and *love* are confused

1

all the time. And, frankly, it's a bit insulting to those of who are holding out for the real thing.

"Hey, M, sorry to keep you waiting. . . ."

I peel my eyes away from the Comatose Love Twins to see Jayson's tall, muscular frame standing over me. He runs his hand through his thick reddish-brown hair, which leaves a few tufts sticking up, and smiles at me with his gold-green eyes. Behind him, I watch two grown women nearly collide as one fixates on his broad shoulders and the other one ogles his blue jeans. As always, Jayson is completely oblivious.

Before you get any weird ideas, let me explain that Jay's my *brother*, and, *no, he's not available*, thank you very much. He's totally in love with his gorgeous, smart, funny (did I mention rich?) girl-friend, Valerie, and believe me, it's for real. In fact, they're probably going to get married. And I'm going to be a bridesmaid. So, for now, you're just going to have to drool.

Jayson twirls the car keys with his fingers. "I couldn't find a parking space. Hope you weren't waiting long."

"It's okay—I had some entertainment," I say wryly, handing him my ten-ton backpack. We hug briefly. Hugging is still a new thing for us—something we started when Jay went away to college last year. I kind of like it. It's a lot better than when we used to wrestle in the den and he'd sit on me, squeezing all the air out of my lungs until I was on the verge of passing out.

A crackly voice comes over the P.A. system to announce a departing bus. Jay presses his lips together and smiles. He looks so much like Mom when he does that. "So how was the trip?"

I could tell him about the charley horse I got in my leg from sitting too long, or the screaming baby across the aisle from me, or even about the mysterious smell of vomit no one could seem to locate—but I don't want Jay to call me a whiner. He's already mistakenly under the impression that since I'm the firstborn girl, I'm a spoiled princess.

"It was great . . . went by just like *that*," I say, snapping my fingers. My fingers, along with the rest of my body, feel coated in a sticky layer of bus slime that I'm praying will melt with a little soap and a strong stream of hot water. "I slept almost the whole way."

Jay flashes me a doubtful smirk. "Val's anxious to see you. I told her we'd meet her for dinner if you're up for it."

"Cool. How are things going with you guys?"

"Fine," Jay answers as we head toward the exit, lumbering under the weight of my pack. "Man, what do you have in here?"

"Stuff," I say. With cramped legs, I struggle to follow alongside my brother. "Can we get burgers tonight? I'm kind of in the mood for a big fat cheeseburger and a side of onion rings."

As Jay opens the door for me, hot Virginia air blasts into the chilled bus station. "Whatever you want, M."

Before we leave, I take one last look over my shoulder at the couple on the bench. Someone should give them a poke to make sure they're still alive. They haven't even moved an inch.

I'm sorry, but that's just not natural.

Heading westbound on I-64, Jay's black Saturn makes the steady climb up Afton Mountain toward Waynesboro. Rocky cliffs rise up to the right of the highway as we near the southernmost tip of Shenandoah National Park. Jay tells me there's a scenic highway nearby called Skyline Drive that follows the crests of the Blue Ridge Mountains for a hundred miles or so. The terrain is so green and beautiful—an endless, graceful chain of gently rolling peaks—so different from the little tree-lined streets of Greenwich, our hometown back in Connecticut. I'm not sure what I was expecting this area to look like, but I never dreamed it would be this stunning. I beg Jay to take a detour up Skyline Drive, but he says it's too late in the day. We'll have to do it some other time.

For now, I have to settle for I-64.

"So Kirsten ditched you?" Jay asks.

I push the seat back to stretch my legs. "She didn't *ditch* me," I answer more sharply than I mean to. The wound is still a little raw, I guess. "She just decided to stay with her mother for a while. They're working some things out."

"That's right—they never did get along too well." He bites his lower lip thoughtfully and thumps his fingers on the steering wheel in time to a song on the radio.

I twirl my long curly hair into a loose knot to get it off the back of my sticky neck. "I mean, I'm glad they're working on their relationship and everything, but why do they have to do it *now?* Can't they wait until after the trip? Am I being totally selfish?"

He raises his thick eyebrows and exhales. "A little, but it's completely understandable, given the situation."

Jay's approval spurs me on. "After all, *she* was the one who asked *me* to go across the country with *her*. . . ." I rant, my blood pressure shooting up ten points. It's hard to think about everything Kirsten put me through these last few weeks without suddenly wanting to crush something to smithereens with my bare hands. I spot one of Jayson's plastic tape cases in the console between our seats. It'll do just fine.

"It's hard when you have to depend on someone else, especially when they're unreliable," Jay says with the voice of experience, even though he's only a year older. He spots me clutching the tape case a bit too tightly and takes it away, keeping one hand on the wheel. "So where does this leave you now? Are you going to give up this travel thing and go to Yale with me in the fall?"

"I don't know yet, *Dad*." I sigh, playing with the frayed edge of my cutoffs instead.

"I'm just asking. . . ."

"I think I'll just hang around here for a while— if that's okay."

"Take as long as you want," my brother says, looking over his left shoulder to pass. "But you should probably make your mind up quick about school. There's a lot of paperwork for incoming freshmen—"

Diversion . . . diversion . . . I need a diversion. . . .

"Jay! What happened to your hand?" I shout, pointing to the tiny white bandage taped over my brother's right palm. "Did you cut yourself?"

Jay glares at me out of the corner of his eye. "It's just a splinter I got when I picked up a two-by-four. It got infected. Don't change the subject."

I groan inwardly. Mom and Dad would be so proud if they could hear the way my brother, Mr. Responsible, was lecturing me right now. Come to think of it, he could be rambling on about the average annual rainfall in Zimbabwe and they'd be proud of that, too.

"You might as well go to college like you'd orig- inally planned," he continues on. "I mean, you're not going to travel by yourself—"

"I don't know," I answer stubbornly. "I might."

"It's not a good idea."

I kick off my boots and peel off my damp socks, letting my toes wriggle free. Jayson discreetly opens the window a crack. "Did I mention Kirsten was disappointed when you weren't there to see me off?" I ask.

Jay knows I'm trying to change the subject again, but for some reason, this time he can't resist. "Oh, yeah?"

"She said she was looking forward to seeing her old 'lab partner' again. How come you didn't tell me you guys were friends in high school?"

Jay shrugs sheepishly. "It was just chem lab, Miranda. It didn't seem important."

"It seemed pretty important to her," I say, needling him. The edges of Jayson's ears are turning red. I'm exaggerating a bit here, just so he'll stop bugging me about school. Like most guys, the topic of women always seems to leave Jay a little flustered. "If I didn't know better, I'd think she had a crush on you."

"Nice try, Miranda." Jay stares intently on the road ahead, his ears turning a deep shade of crimson. "When we get to the apartment, remind me to show you the Yale course catalog. Maybe you'll find something you're interested in."

Or maybe not.

Every spring, Mom and Dad used to grill me, Jayson, and my younger sister, Abigail, about our prospects for getting summer jobs. I used to dread it so much. Abby had a steady baby-sitting gig, so she was usually all set. I procrastinated so much that I always ended up having to make pizzas at Poppa Roni's year after year. Luckily, my best friend, Chloe, got a job there, too, even though she didn't need the money at all, just to keep me company. Still, working was a drag.

And then there was my super-organized brother, Jayson. He would whip out his day planner and show us his mile-long list of job possibilities, contacts, follow-up calls that needed to be made—you name it. My parents were just busting with pride at their Boy Wonder. Now, I love Jay—don't get me wrong—but I still believe that if he hadn't been so gung ho about working during the summer, he could've talked our parents out of making us take jobs. They'll listen to anything he says. I could've spent my summers leisurely reading

9

by Chloe's pool, but thanks to Jay I ended up scraping burned anchovies off the bottom of a nine-hundred-degree pizza oven instead.

"We're here," Jayson says, parking the car in front of a modest brick building with slender white columns and a swath of velvety green grass out front. He cuts the engine. "Welcome to Waynesboro."

A little kid on a red tricycle across the street stops pedaling and looks at us. I wave, and the boy gives me a shy smile, then ducks his head and pedals urgently in the opposite direction.

The apartment is sparsely furnished and impersonal, just like you'd expect of a bachelor pad. There's a sickly beige sofa and two pea-green armchairs, window blinds but no curtains, a warped fake-wood coffee table complete with bubbly water stains, a black torch lamp, and of course— the crown jewel of all bachelor pads—the TV/VCR/stereo entertainment center.

"I like what you've done with the place," I tease.

Jay collapses into one of the pea-green chairs. "All this stuff comes with the apartment, except for the electronics—those belong to Darren."

Through the doorway I can see straight into the kitchen, where Jay's roommate, Darren, is standing in front of the stove stirring something. He's wearing an oversized green T-shirt and a pair of baggy blue jeans that look like they'd be around his ankles if it weren't for the belt holding them up. He seems lost in concentration, staring down into the pan in front of him.

"Do you want to go in and say hi?" Jay whispers, tilting his head toward the kitchen.

I'm feeling a bit shy at the moment, so I tell him I want to settle in and take a shower first. Jay tells me I can leave my pack in his room and leads me up the narrow stairs. The walls are painted a dirty white, with tiny hairline cracks radiating through the plaster like a delicate spiderweb.

"It's not a bad place, really," he insists, reading the look on my face.

"I didn't say anything," I answer innocently.

Jay flashes me one of those I-know-you looks. "The rent's great—it's perfect for the summer."

"Right," I answer cheerfully. "Plus, you're near Val. That's what's important."

"Which reminds me, I'd better let her know we'll be on our way soon." Jayson absentmindedly hustles out of the room and skips down the stairs with the same lopsided rhythm as a galloping horse. As I unpack the crushed clothes in my bag, I can hear him talking in the kitchen with Darren.

Why is Jayson spending the summer living in this drab apartment and building houses? He should be off with Val backpacking through Europe, enjoying life instead of working himself into the ground like Dad.

I worry about my brother.

I worry that sometimes he takes life a little too seriously. I worry that he's so busy always trying to do "the right thing" that he forgets how to have fun. I'd like to tell Jay this, but he'd just brush me off, telling me I need psychiatric help if I'm spending my time worrying about him. The funny thing is, right now I really think it's the only thing that's keeping me from falling apart.

I've just made an exciting scientific discovery—hot water *does* melt bus slime. I have to admit I was a bit afraid the sticky layer of dirt was going to bond permanently to my skin, but now it's all gone. Right down the drain.

It's amazing how a hot shower, a fresh (relatively) pair of khaki shorts, and a tank top can suddenly change your outlook on life. Already, the bus trip, that creepy incident with Richard back in New Jersey, and that horrible fiasco with Kirsten are being conveniently packed away in the back of my mind, not to be recalled again until one day in the distant future when I'm at a dinner party and I'm desperate for an interesting story to tell. Maybe then I'll be able to have a good laugh about it. Or maybe not.

Jayson's waiting for me in the kitchen, chatting it up with Darren. I hover in the doorway for a few seconds, feeling myself shrink inside. Darren's back is turned. Should I say something or wait for Jay to introduce me? Why is meeting people so hard sometimes?

Jay motions for me to come in. "Darren, this is my sister Miranda," he says casually. "Miranda, this is Darren."

"Hi," I answer, timidly walking into the kitchen. As I get closer, I can see what Darren's been stirring all this time—a pot of macaroni.

"Hi, Miranda." Darren regards me with his friendly blue eyes, then awkwardly takes my hand in his crushing grip. "I hear you're going to crash with us for a while."

"Yeah . . . I hope it's okay," I answer, flexing my pulverized fingers behind my back.

Darren slurps macaroni off the wooden spoon and chews it pensively. "It's fine with me, just as long as you can stand living with *this* guy," he says, pointing to my brother.

"I did it for eighteen years," I say. "A few more weeks won't make much of a difference."

Darren lets out a high-pitched, manic burst of laughter that disappears even quicker than it came. It's the kind of laughter that frays nerves and sets off car alarms. His brownish-blond hair is close-cropped and almost woolly in texture—the kind of hair that grows either straight up or horizontally, defying the laws of gravity.

Jay's lips curl into a pained smile. He looks like he wants to laugh with us, but he's too irked that it's at his own expense.

"Just kidding," Darren snorts, shooting Jay a sheepish sidelong glance. "Even Miranda knows

I'm kidding. You know I'm kidding . . . right, Miranda?"

"Sure." I nod at my brother, giving him my best wide-eyed, don't-be-mad look. "We're just having a little fun."

"I know," Jay says with a forced laugh. "I can take a joke—I just didn't think the joke was that funny."

Darren gets back to his macaroni, and I plop down at the kitchen table, doodling in the margins of the *Daily News Leader* with a ballpoint pen. When Jay isn't looking, we exchange quick, mischievous glances, like school kids in detention. I like Darren already.

"Gary called while you were out," Darren says soberly while Jay neatly puts away the clean dishes still draining in the dish rack.

"What's up?" my brother asks.

"He said the hardware store has a bunch of discontinued paint colors they want to donate and maybe a few scraps of linoleum. He thinks there might be enough for the house."

Jay pauses, gripping the dinner plate in his hand like he's an Olympic discus thrower. "That's fantastic! Is it a decent color, at least?"

"Gary didn't say. If it's really bad, they can either mix it or paint the trim with it. We'll find a use for it."

"With the amount of donations pouring in, it looks like we're keeping pretty close to schedule."

"Leann's going to be really happy to hear it." Ripping into a white packet, Darren violently shakes out the sauce mix into the pot of macaroni, sending an atomic dust cloud of orange cheese powder hovering over the white stove top. He breathes in the dust, then lets out a convulsive sneeze.

"Who's Leann?" I ask.

"The woman we're building the house for," Jay explains.

Darren rifles through the Food Lion grocery bag on the counter. "Oh, man!" he says, checking the refrigerator. "I forgot to buy milk!"

"I'd lend you some, but I'm all out, too," Jay says.

"I'll think of something. . . ." Darren's forehead wrinkles as he buries his head in the bare kitchen cabinets. Seconds later he emerges victorious, holding a bottle of salad oil.

"You're *not* using that." My stomach lurches as Darren unscrews the cap.

"Just a little to moisten it," he says. "It'll be fine."

"Nasty," Jay moans while he watches the oil dribble into the pot.

Darren tastes the sloppy mixture and smacks his lips thoughtfully like a master chef searching for the perfect balance of spices. "It's a little thick," he announces, then heads over to the sink to add a healthy dose of tap water. "That should do it."

Jay and I exchange frightened glances and silently agree that it's time to take off.

"We'll see you later," Jay says, opening the back door.

"You're not going to stay for dinner?" Darren pouts. "I've made enough for everyone."

I hold back an overwhelming desire to gag.

"Thanks, but Miranda's in the mood for a burger," Jay says. "You're welcome to join us. It's not too late to save your stomach."

Darren has just discovered a jar of sliced jalapeños in the fridge and is now tossing them into the mixture. "Are you kidding? This is going to be great."

At the very least, you've got to admire the guy's optimism. With a shrug and a wave, Jay and I leave in search of some real food.

Does anyone want some pie?" I ask, pushing my wedge of coconut cream across the booth toward my brother and Valerie. I don't know what I was thinking, ordering it after the burger and onion rings. One bite and suddenly I'm at maximum capacity.

"No thanks," Jay says, absentmindedly twirling a limp French fry in a puddle of ketchup. His eyelids are drooping like he's about to fall asleep sitting up.

My brother's girlfriend tosses her dark hair over one shoulder and grabs a fork. "Hand it over."

To look at her tiny frame, you'd think she never ate anything at all, but Val's got this killer metabolism that burns up everything like a furnace. I think it has something to do with her seemingly endless supply of energy. The first time I met her was when Jay brought her home for Thanksgiving. You should've seen the look on my mom's face when we were all sitting around waiting for dessert, watching Val polish off the rest of the stuffing, the mashed potatoes, and an enormous slab of turkey. Then, after dinner, while the rest of us stretched out in the living room, moaning about our overstuffed bellies, Val was bouncing around, trying to organize a game of touch football.

"So tell me about this Habitat for Humanity thing," I ask Jay, tossing a wadded-up paper napkin onto my plate. "I don't really get how it works."

"It's a nonprofit organization that helps disadvantaged families purchase their own homes," he says in a way that tells me he's had to explain it a thousand times before. "We raise money and get donations from business for the building supplies, then volunteers get together to build the house. The families who have been chosen must donate a certain number of hours to building their house as well as someone else's, and when the job is done, they get to purchase their new house with low payments they can afford."

"Sounds cool," I say, watching Val lick whipped cream off the back of her fork.

Jay's chest expands proudly. "It's a really great program," he says, looking more awake. "For a lot of people, this is the only way they could ever have a home of their own."

"How do you like building houses?" I ask Valerie.

Valerie looks up from her plate, surprised. "Who, me? Are you kidding? I never go over there. I'm not into that kind of stuff."

Jay's chest deflates a little.

"But I think it's great that you're doing it, Sweetie," Val backpedals, giving Jay a kiss on the cheek. She wipes away a residual smudge of her mauve lipstick with her long, slender fingers and smiles at me, her dark eyes crackling with energy. "You know what I'm in the mood for?" Valerie says. "A round or two of mini-golf."

"Yeah, me too!" I shout. Even though I'm bone-tired from the bus ride, Val's spontaneity is contagious.

"What about you? Are you in?" she asks Jay, mussing up his hair.

Jay clears his throat. "Some of us have to go to work tomorrow morning."

"Some of us don't know how to have any fun," Val zings back. Wrapping her arms around my brother's neck, she plants a soft kiss on his lips, turning him into a mushy little puddle. They are so unbelievably cute together.

"All right," Jay relents, struggling to keep his stern face. "But just one round. I have to get up early."

Valerie picks up her purse. "I'll be right back," she says, giving me a wink before heading to the ladies' room.

I lean against the backrest, blowing bubbles into my water glass with a straw. "Would you mind if I went with you to the work site sometime? I think it might be interesting to watch."

"Sure." Jay flips over the check and digs into his pockets while he crunches ice cubes with his teeth. The sound is about as appealing as fingernails on a blackboard—it makes my teeth hurt right down to the roots. I make an obvious, annoyed face, but he doesn't see me, or at least pretends not to notice. He's too busy counting out change.

"Cheapo."

Jay stares at me, puzzled. "What?"

"You heard me. Cheapo," I say again, tilting the straw into the air. "Is that all you're going to give for a tip?"

He rolls his eyes. "It's ten percent. What do you want from me?"

"Waiting is a tough job."

"And you're speaking from experience?"

"Well, no . . . " I put my glass back down on the table. "But it wouldn't kill you to spread the wealth a little."

"I'm doing volunteer work this summer, M. It's not like I'm exactly rolling in cash right now."

I flash him a doubtful look. Ever since Jay was fifteen, he's been squirreling away his summer earnings and allowances in investments. Don't let him fool you—our little money prodigy's got some bucks.

The lightbulb over my head finally clicks on. I know what this is all about. Grinning, I toss a few bucks of my own on the table.

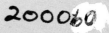

"What's so funny?" Jay asks, grinding another cube into oblivion.

I can feel a smirk twitching at the corners of my mouth. "You're saving up for a ring, aren't you?"

"Ring?" he asks, as if he doesn't know what I'm talking about.

"*Engagement* ring," I say. "You know, for Valerie."

The slack-jawed look on Jay's face right now is absolutely priceless. I've nailed it, and he's totally stunned. I love it when this happens.

"You're way off, Miranda," he sputters, his cheeks turning flush.

Why does he bother denying it? He's my brother—he can't keep any secrets from me. "Am I?"

"We're only sophomores," he argues. "It wouldn't make any sense."

My mind's already flash-forwarded to somewhere in the near future, with Valerie in a long, flowing white gown and me in a gorgeous bridesmaid's dress, carrying a bouquet of roses. She'll be the perfect sister-in-law, taking me shopping or out to lunch, calling me on the phone to commiserate about Jay's quirky habits. But the best part is I know she'll make my brother happy.

"Mom and Dad are going to be thrilled," I gush.

Jay's eyes widen with alarm. "Miranda—"

"Don't worry," I interrupt, putting his mind at ease. "It's our secret."

See that little bump in the middle of the green? Go around instead of over it—you'll get a better shot." Jay gets up from the wooden bench and stands beside me, demonstrating the proper mini-golf swing and follow-through. I might've picked up a pointer or two the first *dozen* times he showed me, but now I'm thinking he's just doing it to show off. Who does he think he is, anyway? Tiger Woods?

"I've got it—I've got it—" I answer, whisking him away like a pesky mosquito. I squint in the glare of the floodlights that gives everything a silvery-orange tint.

"Move your feet apart a little more. . . . "

"Like this?" I say, crushing the green with an exasperated stomp.

"Loosen your grip."

Before my brother has a chance to give me another piece of unsolicited advice, I pull back quickly and give the little red golf ball a solid tap. It follows the path around the molehill like Jay

23

suggested, heading straight for the hole, then takes a sharp, unexpected detour away from it toward the brick border. The ball smacks squarely into the brick, bouncing in the air and rolling out into the walkway leading to the eleventh hole.

"I'll get it," Valerie says, bounding over to a lanky teenage boy who stopped my ball from rolling into the mucky ooze of the small man-made pond. She thanks him with one of her broad smiles and comes skipping back, the boy's eyes glued to the backs of Valerie's slim, tanned legs.

My brother doesn't notice all the attention his girlfriend's getting—he's too busy drawing some sort of bizarre diagram on the back of the score-card. "What you want to do is hit it *here*," he says, referring to the diagram that incorporates a complex series of angles that, when executed correctly, will supposedly result in the perfect shot. Just what I wanted—a geometry lesson.

I beat my putter against the ground. "I thought we came here to have fun." I groan. "I don't feel like *learning* anything."

Jay dejectedly tucks the stubby pencil behind his ear. "Just trying to help you out, M."

"Don't help—just let me play." I feel kind of bad about snapping at him, but if I don't say something now, he'll just keep doing it and I'll go nuts holding it all in. It's not just golf that Jay tries to teach me about; it's everything. It's like he thinks I'm a baby just learning to walk and talk for the first time. He thinks I can't do anything for myself.

Don't forget, Jay, I'm only a year younger than you.

Valerie places the ball on the putting line for me. "I keep telling Jay he should go into teaching. He just loves telling people what to do," she says with an affectionate jab. Jay ignores both of us, tallying the scores so far.

Lining up the shot, I try to incorporate some of the stuff Jay was telling me, but I don't do everything, so he'll know I'm still my own person. I even have my own personal cheering section with Valerie clapping and jumping in the air. I close my eyes, take a deep breath, and then a mischievous thought hits me—instead of the red golf ball, I picture Kirsten's shrunken head at my feet, rolling down the green. . . .

"Remember to go around," Jay whispers, unable to help himself.

Smack. Kirsten's head flies cleanly over the hill, becoming airborne. It's closer to the cup this time, but traveling way too fast to make it. Valerie jumps in front of the ball and stops it with her torso like a soccer goalie. As the ball rolls down Valerie's leg, she daintily points her sandal-clad foot, and it falls right into the cup.

"Hole in one!" I screech and run up to Val, who gives me a high five. Scattered applause breaks out from the surprisingly long line of golfers who are waiting for us to move on to the next hole. Even my brother, Mr. Stuffy, can't help but laugh.

"Good shot," he says, patting me on the back.

"Val gets the assist," I say, dancing with my putter. "Don't forget to put a "1" on that scorecard for me, Jay."

"I would, except it took you fourteen tries to get it into the hole. Lucky for you, there's a six-stroke maximum."

Details . . . details . . .

Jay pats me on top of the head, then puts a big fat "6" next to my name.

If you *really* have to know, Jay won. No surprises there. Valerie won a free game on the last hole by driving the ball up a narrow ramp and into a tiny square at the top of the box. And I got . . . well, don't even ask.

On the way to dropping off Val at her friend Nicole's house, I stretch my legs out in the back seat and lean my head against the window, looking up at the night sky. It's been a long day. Early this morning I was in Cape May, New Jersey, eating breakfast with the locals, then jumping on a ferry to Delaware. And last night I was sleeping in a dark, stinky horse stable with a broken pitchfork by the bed in case any psychos felt like dropping by for a visit. It's only been a few weeks since I left home, but I feel stronger somehow. Already I have a few little notches on my belt of experience—with or without Kirsten.

Val's talking, but I can't make out the words. The sound of her voice, combined with the vibration of the window, lulls me into a sleepy state somewhere between waking and unconsciousness. Despite the peacefulness of the moment, a single, nagging thought rises to the surface. . . .

So, you made it to Virginia. Now what?

Visiting Jay wasn't something I'd planned, but when Kirsten changed her mind at the last minute about going cross-country with me, it seemed like the only reasonable thing to do. Unable to decide if I should go to college or continue the trip alone, I figured staying with Jay would buy me a little time, if not the whole summer, to make up my mind.

It's times like these when I really miss Chloe. Graduation is like a big tornado, sucking people out of your life, then scattering them in a million different places. Sometimes it feels good to have a clean break from your old school friends—it frees you up to meet new people who have no preconceived idea of what you're all about, who just take you at face value without attaching twelve years of judgment to everything you do. Then, other times, you think it would be pretty good to just be sitting in fourth-period study hall again, waiting for the bell to ring so you can ask your best friend advice over dingy lunch trays of scooped mashed potatoes and Day-Glo gravy, confident she'll say exactly what you need to hear.

Knowing Chloe since—well, *forever*—I already have an idea of what she'd say about my current dilemma. *"There's no point worrying about it,"* she'd say so decisively that I'd have no choice but to believe her. *"When the time comes, the decision will make itself."*

Which, I suppose, is another way of saying that if you wait long enough, your options disappear and the choice gets made *for* you, whether it's good or bad. Chloe's one of those people who live by mottoes—little rules for living she swears will solve every problem a person could have. As a result, she almost never worries about anything. It seems a little weird, I know, but Chloe's system really seems to work for her. I, on the other hand, prefer to deal with things on a more flexible, case-by-case basis. The more agonizing and obsessing, the better.

This time, though, I'm thinking of trying it Chloe's way. I won't be totally passive about where my life is headed, but I'm not going to stress about it, either. There could be tons of opportunities for me here in Virginia—stuff I've never dreamed of before. I'll sit back and see what happens. Something will break soon. Something will point me in the right direction. I know it.

All I have to do is keep my eyes open.

Come on, M—it's time to get up."

I'm not sure *why* Jayson is standing over me, tugging annoyingly at my big toe, but if I play possum long enough, maybe he'll give up and go away. I'm maddeningly good at it. So good, in fact, that my sister, Abigail, almost called the paramedics once. Since then, I've learned to throw in a little snore or two so as not to alarm anyone.

"I know you're faking," Mr. Know-It-All says in a singsong voice. "If you get up right now, I'll give you a hundred dollars."

Like *that's* going to happen. Who does this guy think he's dealing with? I snore loudly and roll over.

"Okay, fine," he says, letting go of my toe. "I wanted to be nice, but you leave me no choice. . . . "

While I'm debating whether or not to risk stealing a peek, I feel the whispery sensation of fingertips tickling the soles of my feet.

"WHAT ARE YOU DOING?" I squeal, kicking the blankets off the couch in an involuntary series of froglike convulsions and rubbing the soles of my feet furiously against the carpet to make the tingling disappear. Jay jumps back out of the way, laughing the whole time. The violent transition from gentle sleep to physical torture makes my head feel like it's going to explode. "That's a rotten way to wake up somebody, you know!"

Smirking, Jay regards me with a complete lack of sympathy. "You were already awake!"

I find a dirty, balled-up sock on the floor and hurl it at him. "Well, I wasn't ready to open my eyes yet."

A dull light glows around the edges of the blinds. There's no clock nearby, but I know in my gut that it's some frighteningly early hour I'd rather not see. Jay grins at me with all the nauseating, pink-cheeked freshness of a morning person.

"You're a freak," I say grumpily, letting my heavy head drop back on the pillow. "How long have you been up?"

"Since six. I don't like to start the day rushed."

"Neither do I," I mumble, shooing him away. "So why don't you go play with some hammers and let me get a few more hours in."

"I can't."

"Why not?"

"Because you're coming with me," he says.

I shake my messy head so hard, a few of the tangled curls get caught in my mouth. "Not today," I answer, spitting them out.

Jay folds his arms in front of him. "You said you wanted to visit the site."

"I'm going to be here awhile. Does it have to be today?" I pull the blankets back over the couch and snuggle under. "I'm not a spontaneous person. I need to plan these things."

"It'd be a good day for you to come," he insists. "Darren's not feeling too well. He's staying home."

"The mac and 'cheese'?"

"Yep." He wrinkles his nose. "He was up half the night."

Yuck. My stomach hurts just thinking about it.

Jay's face suddenly morphs from a look of disgust to one of his trademark, ultrasincere, I'm-such-a-good-guy-how-could-you-ever-refuse-me? looks. Already, I know I'm in a heap of trouble.

"You know, we could really use your help, M." I don't have a clue how he does it, but Jay's actually figured out a way to make his dark eyebrows form this sad little tent over his eyes. The guy should go into politics. One sad little tent and a close-up shot beamed to every TV in America, and I swear my brother could run for president.

"*If* I went with you—and I'm only saying *if*— what would I have to do?"

He suppresses a victorious smile. "You know, odds and ends—whatever needs to be done. You'll have fun. Trust me."

I shoot Jay a dirty look and don't say anything for a few minutes, so he knows I'm making this

32

decision on my own and not because he made his eyebrow tent. "I don't have anything to wear," I say finally.

"You can borrow these," he says, handing me an old pair of jeans and a yellow T-shirt covered with splotches of white paint.

Sighing, I grab the clothes out of his hand. "Why do you always have to be so *prepared* all the time?"

"It's my job," Jay says, grinning. "Hurry up. Your ride leaves in ten minutes."

While Jay orders us some coffee at the Hardee's drive-through, I try to steal a few winks. The irritatingly perky radio guy says it's going to be a beautiful day—clear, sunny, and *hot.* It's only eight o'clock in the morning, and already my neck is damp with sweat and Jay's oversized T-shirt is sticking to my back. Just wait until the midday sun hits—that's going to be a real treat.

Jay nudges me. "Be careful—it's hot," he says, handing me my coffee.

Great. Just what I need right now. Boiling coffee.

"Can you turn the air on? I'm dying here." As soon as I take the first sip, beads of sweat immediately form on my upper lip.

Jay snickers, then turns the air conditioner on full blast.

"What's so funny?" I ask, positioning all the blowers in my direction. One of them I strategically place to cool down my scorching coffee.

"I'm picturing you at the site, asking one of the

crew leaders to fan you with a palm frond because you're too hot."

I scowl. "Look, I didn't *ask* to come along on the hottest day of the year. Excuse me if I don't enjoy being roasted like a peanut."

"I'm just teasing—lighten up," Jay says in between sips of coffee. "It's going to be a great day."

Twenty minutes later, we're driving down a small residential street flanked with small, one-story homes on either side. It's your average, middle-class American neighborhood, with minivans and swing sets, houses so close together that you can open your window and have a conversation with your next-door neighbor while she washes her car. Growing up, I thought many times it would be fun to live in a place like this, where there were a lot of kids. Our house, like most of the places in Greenwich, is on a good-sized piece of land, secluded by trees, hedges, and stone walls. It's pretty and private, but you can't exactly step outside your door and be in the center of activity.

The pavement ends abruptly, and the road turns to gravel as we reach the dead end, which stops right in front of a wooded, undeveloped area. To the left of us are two brand-new houses, each with small front porches and landscaped walkways. The design is simple, but cozy. On the other side of the street are two empty lots—one that hasn't been cleared yet, and one in the beginning stages of construction.

Jayson points to the two finished houses. "Those two Habitat houses were finished before I got here. That one"—he motions to the cleared lot on the other side—"is the house we're working on now."

"Is it going to look like the other two?"

"Not exactly, but similar."

A bunch of people are already at the site, standing around, talking. They all look so bright-eyed and enthusiastic. *Ugh. Just what I need in my life . . . more sickeningly happy morning people.*

Reaching into the back seat, Jay retrieves two tool belts, laying one of them in my lap. "This is Darren's, but you can borrow it," he says, then puts on his own.

A heavy cloud of dread settles in the middle of my chest as I stare down helplessly at the tools. Other than the hammer and the measuring tape, I don't know what any of these things are called, let alone what they're for. Even from a distance I can tell that the people in the crew know what they're doing. I haven't left the car yet and already I feel like an idiot.

"Why did you make me come here?" I groan, trying in vain to figure out how to put the belt around my waist.

Jay fixes it for me. "You think you can stay with me for free? You have to pay your rent somehow," he says with a wink.

Gee, thanks for your generosity, bro.

Jay jogs over to the site, with me trailing fifty

feet behind. The leather belt is heavy, and the hammer's handle bounces annoyingly against the side of my thigh. My hips feel huge. The sun is beating down hotly on the top of my damp head, so I throw on an old baseball cap, pull my hair through the hole in the back, and put on a pair of sunglasses. In addition to protecting me from the sun, the hat's visor and the dark glasses make me feel like I'm in my own little world. I might just prop myself against a tree with a hammer in my hand and take a nap. No one will be the wiser.

Kneeling on the ground, I tie and retie the laces on my hiking boots several times, trying to waste a few minutes. Jay's talking to a tall, beefy man with dark curly hair and a mustache. He waves at me to come over. I stop dawdling and trudge across the lawn to where he's standing.

"Miranda, this is Gary, our crew leader," Jay says, introducing us. "Gary, this is my sister."

"Nice to meet you," Gary says in a booming voice. He's wearing a red T-shirt that says GARY'S CONSTRUCTION in white iron-on lettering. When he extends his hand, I expect him to crush my fingers in his grip, like Darren did, but Gary's handshake is surprisingly gentle. "It's great to have you onboard, Miranda. You like building houses?"

"I don't know—I've never done it before."

"That's all right," he says. "You can hammer a nail, can't you?"

In front of us, the gray walls of the foundation

rise crisply out of the ground, like a miniature, rectangular version of the Great Wall of China. I may not know anything about building houses, but I'm sure it must take a bit more skill than pounding nails to make a foundation. "You know, I've never been very good with tools," I gush nervously. "I once tried to hang a picture in my room and ended up smashing a hole through the wall. I can see that you guys do some really great work here, and I don't think you want someone like me around, messing things up."

Gary takes off his baseball cap and scratches the back of his head. "We don't have any walls yet, so it looks like you're going to be okay."

Just as I begin to mention my paralyzing fear of circular saws, Jay claps his hand forcefully on my shoulder. "Miranda's not that bad. She's just being modest. Aren't you, Miranda?"

I don't say anything.

Gary's round face softens. "Don't worry about it if you don't know what to do," he says. "Most of the people you see here didn't know how to build, either. We'll show you everything you need to know, and I'm sure your brother will be glad to guide you if you need help."

The corners of my grumpy mouth tug into a reluctant smile. "Great."

Jay points me in the direction of a blue beach cooler filled with ice and jugs of water. "Make sure to drink lots of water—in fact, you might as well get started now. We wouldn't want you passing out on us."

While I'm guzzling water like my life depends on it, Gary gathers everyone into a circle. He starts going over the day's agenda, talking about such exotic things as tie extensions, sealants, and grade lines. A lot of people in the group are nodding their heads, including my brother, which makes me wonder if they really know what Gary's talking about or if they're too embarrassed to admit they don't know what's going on.

"You'll find the brushes over by the lumber pile," Gary drones on.

My watch says eight forty-five. *God, it's early.* I take a seat on top of the cooler and contemplate all the things I could be doing today instead of being here. I could maybe sleep in, watch a little TV, take a walk and check out a few stores nearby, have lunch, stretch out on the lawn and read, take a nap . . . heck, I'd even be willing to clean Jay's apartment for him. I wish I'd thought of that sooner. He might've actually gone for it.

"And we have a new volunteer. Miranda Burke—Jay's sister—visiting from Connecticut."

My ears perk up like a dog's when I hear my name. I'm midguzzle when the whole group turns to look at me, slouching lazily on top of the water cooler. It's a scene right out of one of my worst nightmares. With a mortifying trickle of water streaking out of the corner of my mouth, I raise my paper cup in the air and give the group a feeble salute.

Gary leads everyone in a short prayer, then the crew scatters and gets right to work. I decide to pour myself another cup of cold water. Like Jay said, I wouldn't want to get dehydrated.

"Miranda?"

Looking up from the water jug, I see a very tan guy in cutoffs staring down at me through his blond bangs. "I'm T. J. ," he says, offering me his hand.

"Nice to meet you, T. J. ," I answer, eyeing him from behind my shades.

"You're Jay's sister?"

I give him a coy grin. "Yeah, but you won't hold it against me, will you?"

"I'll try not to," he says with a smile that reveals his slightly crooked but completely adorable teeth. "Has anyone shown you around the site yet? Would you like a tour?"

Now *this* is worth getting up early for.

"Sure," I say as I hop off the cooler, hoping I don't look *too* eager. "Lead the way."

Out of nowhere, Jay suddenly materializes, his brotherly eyes shifting from T. J. to me and back again. "Gary needs you by the lumber pile, T. J. ," he says, his voice dropping a few octaves. "Miranda, come with me."

T. J. gives me a smile. "Maybe later?"

"Yeah—" I was going to add that I was looking forward to it, but Jay is already pushing me away, shoving a wide paintbrush in my hand. "Are you going to chase away *every* guy who talks to me, or just the cute ones?" I ask, following Jay to the other side of the foundation.

Jay pries the lid off a ten-gallon bucket, refusing to look at me. "I didn't chase anyone away. We need to get to work, that's all."

Yeah, right.

"You're going to help seal the basement," he continues on, like one of those home repair guys on TV. "It's to keep water from seeping in. Just dip the brush in here and spread it on."

With arms stubbornly folded in front of me, I stare at my brother as he stirs the sealant with a wooden stick. "How?"

Jay takes my brush and shows me a few test strokes. His face is slightly flush—I can tell he's enjoying the opportunity to teach me something new. "Pretend you're painting a fence," he says.

"Just make sure to cover the concrete well."

"It smells really bad." I hold my breath as I watch him spread on the thick goop. "I bet those toxic fumes are dangerous."

Jay rolls his eyes. "The container says it's fine as long as you use it in a well-ventilated area. You can't get any better ventilation than being outside, Miranda." I can tell his patience is wearing thin.

"And you believe that?" I ask incredulously. "Ten years from now they're going to discover that the fumes from this stuff released into the atmosphere is what's responsible for all those mutant frogs they're finding with five legs. If it can mutate a frog, just imagine what it can do to your sister!"

"Well, if you grow an extra arm, then you'll be able to get twice as much sealing done," Jay deadpans. "I'll be inside the foundation if you suddenly need another paintbrush."

He hands me back the brush and walks off. Frozen, I stand there with it poised in midair, watching a thick black pearl of sealant slowly roll down the handle.

Jay suddenly stops in his tracks and turns around. "One more thing, M—"

"What?" I snap.

"Try to be a little more enthusiastic about the project, will you? A good attitude makes all the difference."

I shrug. "Yeah, whatever."

If you've ever seen one of those old prison movies where the sweaty convicts are lined up, slaving away under the searing rays of the sun, then you have some idea of what it's like to be me right now. Instead of mining coal with a pickax, though, I'm slathering this weird, rubbery stuff against a big gray wall. I've only covered a two-foot-square area, and already my shoulder's starting to ache, plus my throat burns from the fumes. On top of that, my bladder's on the verge of bursting from all the water I've drunk.

I stare sullenly at the tiny patch I've covered so far and decide it's time for a break.

"Where's the bathroom?" I whisper to Jay through one of the window holes in the foundation.

He shakes his head. "Already?"

"Come on," I say urgently, bobbing up and down. "Where is it?"

"See that green Portosan on the other side? That's it."

Ya-hoo . . . a portable toilet. Can this day get

any better? *Look at the bright side,* I tell myself as I trudge over to the outhouse, *at least you don't have to wear those horrible prison uniforms.*

When I return to my paintbrush and goop, there's an athletic-looking woman in a tank top sealing the wall only a few feet away from my spot. The tightly coiled bun on the back of her head wobbles as she moves. I swear I haven't been gone more than five minutes, and in that time she's covered more than twice the area I have, painting it on with broad, smooth strokes instead of my stiff, deliberate ones.

"Hi, there. I'm Marcy—you're Miranda?" she says.

"Yeah." I try to inject a little enthusiasm in my voice, but I don't think it's getting across. Marcy doesn't stop to shake my hand or anything—she's all business. At the rate she's going, I think she'll have our whole side done before lunch. "So, how's it going?" I say, struggling to make small talk.

"Pretty good," Marcy answers, never taking her eyes off her brush. "The foundation came out great, didn't it?"

"Oh, yeah—it's a beauty," I say, half-joking. How would I know the difference between a good basement and a crummy one?

"We were afraid there'd be a lot of air pockets because the guy who poured the concrete didn't seem to know what he was doing."

I pick up my brush and try to imitate Marcy's

44

movements. "If he didn't know what he was doing, then why did you hire him?"

"We didn't hire him—he volunteered," she says, her muscular arms glistening in the sun. "Almost everything is done by volunteers. Gary, the crew leader, has his own construction business. He does this stuff in his free time."

You couldn't pay me a million dollars to do this for a living, I think wryly to myself. Yet, strangely enough, here I am, spreading goop on the walls of a basement—for free.

"So you're in construction, too?" I ask.

Marcy seems disturbed by my brushing technique and takes a moment to give me a little fine-tuning. "Relax that wrist. You're too stiff."

I find myself complying without hesitation, the way a soldier jumps when a drill sergeant gives orders. Pretty soon I'm speeding along to Marcy's satisfaction, and she answers my question.

"No—actually, I'm a junior high physical education instructor," she says in a voice touched with the faintest hint of a southern accent. "This is what I do during the summer."

While my brush zips across the concrete, Marcy tells me about everyone in the crew. There are a few college students, like my brother and Darren, several people from a local church group—T. J. being one of them—an electrician, a roofer, and a family who is applying for a Habitat house of their own. In all, there's about fifteen people on the crew.

"What about you?" Marcy finally asks. "What do you do?"

The question stops me cold. It used to be that, at the very least, I could tell people I was a high school student. Or, if I wanted to make my life more exciting, I would add that I was planning on attending Yale after graduation. And even when I changed my mind about college I was able to say that I was going to travel the country to see where life would take me. But things have changed. Not only do I no longer have any big plans or prospects, I have no direction, either. I can't be categorized. Never in my life has the question *What do you do?* been so loaded and so complicated.

"Well," I finally answer with a deep sigh, "right now I'm sealing a basement."

In between brush strokes I steal glances at Marcy's watch, counting the long, painful seconds until lunchtime. It feels like years before noon comes. At twelve on the dot, the crew takes refuge in the shade of the uncleared trees on the adjacent lot, sitting on the ground all clustered together while they eat their lunch and ramble on about the next phase of building. Don't these people talk about anything else?

Away from the group, I find a big, old tree on the edge of the lot with thick roots that spread out at the base in a sort of U-shape. Jay comes along with two brown paper bags as I slump tiredly against the tree. He tosses me one of the bags and sits down.

"I don't think I can lift my arms to eat." I sigh, looking inside my bag. Tuna salad on a pita, apple, iced tea.

Jay narrows his eyes and looks at me from side to side. "Where's that third arm I thought you were supposed to get?"

"I chopped it off trying to kill myself," I say, taking a miserable bite out of my sandwich. Even in the shade the air's so thick and hot, it's hard to breathe. "After lunch, why don't you take me back to your apartment? I've already worked half a day, and besides, I'm not really much use here. . . . " In order to persuade Jay even more, I attempt to make my eyebrows tent like he does. The look we're going for here is *wretched anguish.* But judging from the twisted grin on my brother's face, I'd say I achieved something more along the lines of *maniacal facial tic.*

"If I take you back, it'll take at least an hour," he says. "That's too much work time lost."

"I'll take a nap in the car, then."

"It's too hot in there." Jay rips into a bag of tortilla chips and offers me some. "You'd suffocate. You know what happens to a dog when it's left in a hot car—its brain expands, and it dies. If that can happen to a dog, just imagine what can happen to you."

He's trying to be funny. I hate it when he tries to be funny.

"I'll turn on the air-conditioning," I answer stubbornly.

"And overheat my car? I don't think so."

Gritting my teeth, I'm about to throw out the lunch bag, but find something else inside. "A brownie?" I say, my hard scowl instantly dissolving. "You got me a brownie?"

"It looked like something you'd go for," he says modestly. "It's got frosting on it."

Nothing can make you feel more like a jerk than an unexpected act of kindness, especially when it comes at a time when you haven't exactly been acting your best. Sheepishly, I unwrap the brownie and take a bite off the corner. It's really great.

Several members of the crew are already back on their feet, tossing their trash in garbage cans and heading over to the foundation for an afternoon of more self-inflicted punishment. T. J. glances my way, but once he sees my brother sitting next to me, he turns on his heel and walks in the other direction.

"I don't know if you remember this or not," Jay says after taking a long pull from his bottle of iced tea, "but when I was around twelve or so, Mom and Dad thought it would be a good idea for me to have a paper route. I said okay, not really realizing what was involved, and once I got started, I absolutely hated it. Every day after school, instead of hanging out with Brian and Eddie, I had to pass papers. It took a couple of hours at least, and in the winter even longer because I couldn't ride my bike in the snow."

A light of recognition flashes in my mind. "Oh, yeah—I remember something about you coming home from school once and hiding in the attic. Mom couldn't find you and ended up having to deliver the papers herself."

Jay's shoulders shake with laughter. "Boy, did I get in a load of trouble for that. I asked Mom and Dad to let me quit the route, but they said I'd made a commitment and I had to stick to it. After a while, when I realized there was no getting out of it, I decided that the only thing I could do was change my attitude. So I pulled this Toys 'R' Us flyer out of one of the papers and started thinking about some of the things I could save up for with my paper route money. Suddenly, the job wasn't just something Mom and Dad were making me do. It was something I was doing for myself. Every paper I delivered got me closer to the video game or the basketball I wanted."

"And your point is—"

"From that moment on, I realized I could be miserable or happy in any situation. It all depended on how I chose to see it," Jay says.

I take another bite from my brownie, choosing to ignore the obvious reference Jay is making to my current outlook on life. "You'd better marry Val soon, Jay. You don't even have kids yet and already you're sounding like a dad. You've got the lectures down and everything."

"I wouldn't call it a *lecture*," he says. "It's just really good for you to know that you have a choice between being unhappy or making the best of a situation."

"Do I have to go to my room now?"

"*No—*" Jay gets to his feet and wipes the

crumbs off his work pants. "But it'd be nice if you could finish out the day, M. We really need all the help we can get."

"No problem," I say, taking the smallest nibble humanly possible off the corner of my brownie. "I'll get right back to work as soon as I'm done with my lunch."

The blistering afternoon wears on at a snail's pace. I pick a spot near Marcy, who, in between stretches of silent, focused work, tells me a few stories about her students and the softball team she coaches after school. Jay, my parole officer, shows up around five o'clock, and we head for the car, bone-tired and dried out by the sun. As repetitive and insignificant as the work seemed to be, even I have to admit the crew seemed to accomplish an awful lot in one day. I guess it feels sort of good to think that I was part of that.

"I'll see you tomorrow!" Marcy says, still spreading on the sealant. She's one of the diehards who likes to put in a little extra time.

Don't count on it, I think to myself, waving.

Once I unload the silly tool belt and sink into the passenger seat, all is right with the world again. Jay and I don't talk most of the way back to his apartment. My brother doesn't have to say a word—I can *feel* his disapproval hanging over me like a wet, smothering rag. A subtle glimmer of self-satisfaction colors his cheeks, as if once again he was right about me. I'm just a fragile, spoiled little princess who'll never do anything *serious* with her life.

"I hope you weren't expecting to go somewhere tonight," Jay says tiredly. "If you want to do something, we could rent a movie."

"Are you kidding?" I scoff. "I'm wiped out. I'd probably fall asleep during the opening credits."

Jay tunes the radio to a financial talk show on a crackly AM station. The host has a flat, droning voice like Mr. Pritchard, my old calculus teacher. First I had to hear about basements all day, and now I'm being subjected to advice on selecting the right mutual fund. All this adult talk is making me numb. My mind is sliding rapidly into a paralyzing, drooling coma.

"Tomorrow's going to be another long day at the site," Jay says during the commercial break. "You'll probably want to go to bed early."

My blistered fingers dig deep into the plastic armrest. Jay's a smart guy, but sometimes when reality is staring him in the face, he tends to look the other way.

"You know, Jay," I say as clearly and deliberately as I can, "I think it's really cool that you enjoy all this building stuff—it's a great cause and everything—but I'm just not cut out for it."

"Yeah? Well, I thought you were doing pretty

good by the end. You looked like you were really getting into it."

I roll down the window and rest my arm on the ledge. "Actually, I was, a little. But *very* little."

Jay's nodding sympathetically, but the blank expression on his face tells me he still isn't getting it. "I know the first day can be tough—but it really does get easier. You'll see."

"No, I won't—I don't want to go with you tomorrow." Nervously, I chew on the inside of my lower lip, waiting for him to say something. *It's just Jay*, I keep telling my hot, churning stomach. *Who cares if you don't want to build houses with him? You don't have to like the same things. It's no big deal.* But if it's no big deal, why am I going through the same nerve-jangling anxiety I felt when I told my parents I didn't want to go to Yale?

Of course Jay's much cooler than my parents were, but unfortunately he's just as determined to change my mind. "I hate to see you give up on something so fast, M, without really giving it a chance."

"I think eight hours is more than enough time to know if you want to continue with something or not."

Jay shakes his head. "Trust me, I can tell you from experience that one day is not enough to get an accurate—"

"Experience?" I shout. "Jay, you're only a year

and a half older than me! I'm not all that far behind you in the experience department!"

"At this stage in life, a year and a half *is* a big difference," he says in a voice that is so patronizing, I want to scream. "Plus, I have the benefit of a year of college behind me."

So we're back to college again. . . . I fall silent, having been backed into a corner I can never argue my way out of. Sure, I could explain my philosophy that college should be a choice and not an expectation, or that I believe there are many paths to happiness that don't involve higher education, but no matter what I say, Jay will always be able to throw the college issue in my face.

The burning heat in my stomach dies out, replaced by a sharp coldness. If I don't go to college, it suddenly becomes clear to me, I'll never have my brother's respect.

"I came here to sort things out, not to build a house," I answer in my firmest voice. "I went and saw the site and I did a little work in Darren's place because he was sick. I think that's more than fair, Jay."

"It's not about being fair," he argues as he pulls the car into the driveway. "It's about what's best for you."

What's best for me?

Jay thinks this question has never even popped into my head. What he doesn't know is that it's made hundreds of appearances during tense dinner conversations at home, at after-school crying sessions at Chloe's, and in the middle of many sleepless nights. What he also doesn't know is that I've had this conversation before, in my head, with various opponents, where I eloquently defend my position explaining that "the best" for someone means the one perfect choice that will bring that person perfect happiness. In a world of unlimited possibilities, I don't see how you can know what "the best" is without weighing at least some of the other options.

"So you want what's best for me, huh?" I say, savoring the setup. Poor Jay. He has no idea how long I've been waiting to use this zinger.

"Right," he says, falling perfectly into my trap. "I only want what's best."

"Well, the best thing for me right now is to make my *own* decision. Back off so I can figure it out on my own," I snap, slamming the car door behind me.

Jay pulls one of his stony, I-can't-handle-this-right-now-so-I'm-ignoring-you faces and heads straight for his room the second we get into the apartment. Fine with me. I need a break from him, anyway.

Darren's at it in the kitchen again, pale-faced and weak. For someone who'd made himself sick exactly twenty-four hours ago, you'd think he'd cut his losses and go for something harmless like a bowl of cereal. Nope—not Darren. He's back on the culinary horse, wreaking havoc once again at the stove. This time the crime involves a frying pan, eggs, a few tortillas, and some questionable-looking hamburger. He puts some oil in the hot pan, and when it starts to smoke he adds two eggs and a handful of raw hamburger.

"Are you sure you should be eating that?" I say, watching him stir the mixture into a sickening scramble. "Maybe you should take it easy on your stomach."

Darren squints through the blue smoke. His

lower lids are dark and puffy. "I feel fine now—this is going to be great," he says. "Thanks for going on the site today, by the way. How did it go?"

"It was fine," I say. There's no point in making the guy feel bad for being sick. "I had to put sealer on the foundation walls."

"Sealer, huh? That's a tough one."

"Yeah?"

"It's definitely not my favorite part of the whole process," he says.

I back away a little from the frying pan, which is emitting a strangely sour smell. "So what *is* your favorite part?"

While Darren pauses for a moment and thinks, his greasy spatula drips hamburger-egg juice on the floor. "It's pretty exciting when the walls go up, because you can really see the house starting to take shape. But I also like it when we work on the inside, like laying carpet or hanging wallpaper. The people you're building for get really excited at that point because they know the wait is almost over."

As if his concoction wasn't already bad enough, Darren reaches into the cupboard and pulls out a giant-sized bottle of hot pepper sauce and starts pouring the fiery liquid all over the eggs until they turn pink. A nauseous chill runs through me. After a day like today, I can't afford to have Darren do this to himself again. If he gets sick, it's tool belts and portable toilets for me all over again.

I decide to take matters into my own hands. "Darren, put down the bottle, walk away slowly, and no one will get hurt."

"What?" He looks up at me, puzzled, then accidentally burns his hand on one side of the pan.

I can't believe this guy's parents let him live on his own. He's a disaster waiting to happen. . . . I'm getting a sneaking suspicion that keeping Darren out of harm's way is going to be a full-time job. While he goes to the sink to pour cold water over his wound, I make my move.

"This stuff will burn a hole right through your stomach," I say, swiftly throwing the pink eggs and fuzzy tortillas in the trash. "Let me make you something good."

Darren doesn't protest. In fact, I think he likes the idea of someone cooking for him. He wraps his burned finger in a wet paper towel and sits down at the table. I open the refrigerator and cupboards and look for supplies. There isn't a lot to work with. I steal a ripe tomato and a clove of garlic from Jay's side of the fridge. In the bread box I find a couple slices of dry white bread and put them in the toaster.

"I'm a terrible cook. I love it, but I'm really bad," Darren admits. "Sometimes I watch those cooking shows—you know, the ones where they go to these swank restaurants and the chef is there, throwing stuff together." He flails his arms spastically in the air to illustrate his point, his knobby elbows within inches of smashing into the wall. "They just take whatever's nearby and toss it all together and like two minutes later it's this incredible thing. I just can't figure out how they do it."

"Cooking school," I answer, chopping the tomato into chunks. "I once thought about going to cooking school."

"Yeah?"

"Yeah. I mean, I like cooking, but I'm not so sure I like it *that* much, you know?" In a small bowl I mix together some oil and vinegar that I find in the cupboard, and add in some finely chopped garlic. "If I had to pick, though, I'd choose cooking over sealing basements in a heartbeat."

Darren wads up the wet paper towel and throws it at the trash can across the room. He misses his target by a mile, and the sopping, pulpy mass slaps against the wall like a giant spitball. "You should come back to the site in a few days, when things really start to get fun. You can meet Leann."

I sigh loudly. "You sound like my brother. He's determined to have me spend every waking minute at the site."

"I didn't mean to sound pushy," Darren says apologetically. "You don't have to do it if you don't want to."

Try telling that to Jay.

The toaster pops, and I put the two pieces of

toast on a plate. "How long have you been building with Habitat?"

"Three summers," he says. "This is my fourth house."

"So you like it?"

"It's one of the best things I've ever done. It's hard work, but it's a lot of fun, too."

"That's what I keep hearing," I murmur under my breath. As I put the chopped tomatoes on the toast and drizzle the salad dressing over everything, I'm really starting to wonder if there's something wrong with me for not liking this whole building thing, or if maybe everyone in Augusta County is nutty. It's probably something in the tap water. I make a mental note to pick up some bottled water at Food Lion tomorrow.

I add a pinch of salt and pepper and a sprinkle of oregano that I find in the cupboard, and dinner is served. Darren looks really impressed. "What is that?" he says, turning his plate, looking at it from all sides.

"You can call it *bruschetta* if you want to be fancy, but it's really just an open-faced Italian tomato sandwich."

Darren takes a bite and smiles. "So how long did you say you're staying?"

It's almost midnight, and I'm stretched out on the couch, bound up with blankets like a mummy, except for one loose arm that is freed solely for the purpose of using the TV remote control to its fullest capacity. Even though I'm so tired that my eyes are burning, I can't tear myself away from the hypnotic trance Darren's state-of-the-art TV has put me in. Aside from the fact that it gets practically every channel on the planet, the TV has this feature where you can freeze the picture just by pressing a button. If you hit it just right, you can catch some pretty dignified people making some pretty hideous faces. This little game I've discovered takes TV to a whole new level.

While I'm clicking away, Jay comes downstairs and sits on one of the chairs. "Aren't you hot?" he says, taking a look at my mummified state. "It's probably eighty in here."

"I like the heaviness," I say. I've always been one of those odd people who needs to be buried under piles of blankets no matter what time of year. If I'm not smothered, it's hard to sleep.

Jay looks at the TV while I channel-surf to find someone good to freeze. Secretly, I wish my brother's face was on the screen, in a tight close-up. I bet underneath that controlled facade we could unmask some interesting things.

"So what are you doing tomorrow?" he asks, staring at the TV.

"Who knows?" I hit the button just as a willowy beauty on one of those nighttime soap operas is about to whisper a scathing secret. On the freeze-frame, her seductive upper lip has turned up on itself, and her front teeth have this goofy overbite, like a pit bull on laughing gas.

I crack up, but Jay doesn't even smile. "Maybe I'll do this all day," I say.

"Val said she might call you in the morning to see if you want to do something."

"You asked your girlfriend to baby-sit me?"

"I didn't ask her to do anything," he says sourly. "She offered."

Call me paranoid, but I find it pretty hard to believe it's as innocent as all that. Jay probably convinced Val to lecture me about Yale, as part of his *Save Miranda's Future* project.

"I don't know . . . I might already have plans of my own," I answer coolly.

"You don't have to go—Val just thought you might get bored here by yourself."

On one of the news channels I find an

interview with some old-looking political guy. There are some frightening, screen-filling close-ups of his fleshy face. My finger is poised over the freeze button. It looks like we're about to hit pay dirt.

"I want to talk to you about something," Jay says, sounding all serious. It's amazing how, when I'm not looking at him, I really notice how much his voice sounds like Dad's. It gives me the chills. Do I sound like Mom?

I have to admit I'm somewhat curious about what Jay has to say, but not enough for me to tear my eyes away from the screen. The geezer opens his mouth wide as if to argue a point, and *click*, I capture the moment in all its frozen glory. Mouth twisted grotesquely to one side, jowls caught midsway to the other. Nostrils flaring. Eyes rolling back. On my scale of freaky faces, I'd definitely give this guy 9.5 remote controls out of 10.

"Oh, M," Jay groans, shaking his head. "Please don't do that to the chairman of the Federal Reserve." He takes the remote from me and turns the TV off. "Listen up—I really need to say something."

Ugh. What now?

"Can't it wait until tomorrow?" I say. "I'm kind of tired."

Jay's lips are tightly drawn against his teeth. "I just wanted to apologize for forcing you to work at the site. I shouldn't have been so pushy. I'm sorry."

For a split second, I contemplate making a wisecrack, then I think better of it. This is too huge. I can count on one hand the number of times Jay has apologized to me over the years. It's not that he doesn't know how to say he's sorry— it's just that he's maddeningly right most of the time.

"Sometimes I forget we're two different people," he continues, shifting uncomfortably in his chair. "Just because you're my sister doesn't mean we're always going to be interested in the same things."

"We're almost *never* interested in the same things," I say gently. "We're actually *very* different people, Jay. You fit in well with the rest of the Burkes, but sometimes I'm pretty convinced some redheaded fairy fluttered out of the skies and dropped me on Mom and Dad's doorstep."

For some reason, Jay looks almost hurt. "You're not *that* different."

"I don't mind if we have our own way of doing things. I just hate it when you're convinced that your way is the *only* way."

"You mean about school."

"I mean about everything," I say. "You've got it all down—you know exactly what you want out of life and how to get it. That's great for you, but I don't work that way. I have too many questions that need answering before I can get to where you're at."

65

"And I can help," Jay says earnestly. "I wish I could've had an older brother or sister to guide me. You should feel lucky—you can benefit from my experience without making the same mistakes."

Taking a deep breath, I fix my brother with a patient gaze, searching for the right words to make him understand. "I *want* to make mistakes, Jay. If you're sitting there, warning me of every pitfall, it's like going to the movies with someone who blows the surprise ending. It kills the fun."

"There's more to life than just having a good time." Jay tiredly scratches his chin. "I care about what happens to you, M, and it's hard to stand by and watch you do something you might regret for the rest of your life."

"It's not so much the outcome I'm worried about right now, but the journey," I say, sinking under the covers. "You've had yours—now let me have mine."

As I hum happily to myself over a morning bowl of granola, bits of the previous night's conversation with Jay keep resurfacing, my mind punching up the details with each replay. Boy, I was good. Everything I needed to say came out even better than I'd hoped. I don't know if I was able to convince my brother to treat me more like an adult, but here's a few things I've decided to do to help change his mind:

1) Stop acting like a kid (in front of Jay, anyway). I can beg and plead for my brother to treat me like a grown-up, but I figure that won't change a thing unless I at least try to act the part. This includes buying my own food, cleaning up after myself, and (the tough one) whining as little as possible. I can do that, no problem. And while I'm at it, maybe I'll read up a little on the stock market, so Jay and I can have an intelligent, adult conversation.

Yeah, right.

2) Let Jay help. If it really makes him feel so

important to give me advice, then I might as well let him do it. I mean, what do I care? But instead of waiting around for him to lecture me, I'll be the one to ask the questions—which, if nothing else, allows me to control the subject matter I'm going to be bored by. Then, when he's done talking, I can quietly disregard everything he's said.

3) Make up my mind as soon as possible about what to do next. I wanted to put this off longer, but Jay won't get off my back unless I have some sort of plan in the works. Besides, after what happened yesterday at the site, I'm thinking that taking off isn't such a bad idea after all.

The phone rings, snapping me awake from my granola daydream. "Hello?"

"Miranda? It's Val."

I completely forgot that she was going to call. "Hey, Val. What's up?"

"I'm kidnapping you for the day," she says. "You're not busy, are you?"

"No," I answer honestly. I wonder if I'm going to regret this. "What did you have in mind?"

"I can't tell you. It's a secret."

A sinking feeling settles in the pit of my stomach. "Just tell me one thing—Jay didn't put you up to this, did he? This isn't some sort of trick to get me to go to college, is it?"

Val laughs. "Are you kidding? Trust me—this has nothing to do with school," she says. "It's just you and me bonding. So when can you be ready?"

"I don't know," I say, checking my bed head in the reflection of the microwave. "An hour or so?"

"Great. I'll see you then."

"Wait, what should I wear?"

"Casual clothes," she says. "And bring along a sweater."

"A sweater? It's going to be in the nineties today!"

"Trust me," Val answers mysteriously. "You're going to need it."

Hi there! My name is Valerie, and I'll be your tour guide today," she says, eyes smiling at me from behind a pair of designer shades as I hop into the driver's seat of her little red sports car. "In the interest of safety, we ask that you please buckle your seat belt. Thank you for your cooperation, and enjoy your trip."

Eager to comply, I reach for the buckle. But before it snaps safely into place, Valerie yanks the stick shift in reverse and stomps on the gas, sending us backwards into a tight half-circle. With a hard brake, she shoves the stick in first and we're off, zooming through each successive gear faster than race cars at the Indy 500—Valerie with her wild hair flying out the open window, and me attempting unsuccessfully to join both halves of the seat belt.

"I didn't realize you were wearing cement shoes," I joke as the scenery whips by us in a furious green blur.

Val lets up on the gas a little. "Sorry. I do have

a heavy foot. It runs in the family," she says. "We have a lot of ground to cover, and I want to make sure you see it all."

"So where are we going?" I'm holding my breath as I say this, not entirely convinced that my brother doesn't have a hand in what's going on here. Boy, if this turns out to be a big scheme of his, I'm going to be so ripped. . . .

"You'll find out soon enough," Val says, determined to keep me in suspense. "So Jay's been on your case, huh?"

I laugh bitterly. "Has he been telling you what a misguided loser I am?"

"Not at all," Val answers soberly. "Before he left to pick you up at the bus station the other day, he called right away to tell me you were coming. He was so excited that you were going to be here, he couldn't stop talking about it."

"He's probably happy to have someone to boss around for a while," I answer dryly, wondering how much she's exaggerating. There's no reason in the world for her to make this stuff up, but I don't exactly buy it, either. Jay developing motor-mouth because of my arrival is just as unlikely as a rabbit breaking out into song. It goes against the laws of nature.

"He really thinks the world of you, Miranda," Val says. "But I suppose you already know that."

I'm not sure why it surprises me to hear that Jay's happy to have me around, but it does. "He told me I could stay as long as I wanted, but I thought he was just saying that because I was his sister and he felt obligated. He can be so hard to read sometimes."

"Tell me about it." Val sighs. She falls quiet for several minutes, transfixed by the road and her own thoughts. I get the distinct feeling she wants to say something, but she doesn't know how to broach the subject. "Does he seem different to you?" she finally says, breaking the silence.

"Jay? How do you mean?"

Val shrugs like she already knows the answer. "Is he acting any different than usual?"

I think about it for a minute. "Kind of, I guess. He does seem a little grumpier—but I figured it was me."

"It's not you at all." Val swallows hard. "I think it's me."

"No way," I say, shaking my head.

The corner of Val's mouth quivers with doubt. "He's been weird ever since he got here. I think he's sick of me or something."

Instinctively, I put my hand on hers. "Don't say that. Jay's nuts about you."

"Maybe he was at one time," she says, her voice thick with emotion. "But he doesn't seem to really care anymore. I pushed him into coming here for the summer and now I think he resents me for it."

"It's just the job, Val. I've been at the site and I know how irritating and tiring construction can be—it's probably more work than he thought."

"Jay's never been afraid of hard work," Val insists. "It's something else—something deeper than that. I can see it in his eyes."

Beneath my fingers, I can feel Valerie's hand trembling. *Jay, what've you done to this poor woman?* I wonder to myself. Val's never seemed to me to be the kind of person who would be insecure in a relationship without just cause, and yet, the idea that Jay isn't interested in her anymore is totally ridiculous. At the restaurant, Jay practically told me in not-so-many-words that he wanted to marry Val. How can she possibly think he doesn't love her anymore?

"You're way off base. Really." I say each word heavily, fixing Val with an intense gaze, hoping she catches the full thrust of what I'm trying to say without having to tell her everything. "Trust me— you don't have *a thing* to worry about."

"How can you know for sure?" She sniffles, keeping her eyes on the road.

"I just know." It's torture watching Val's crumbling face, wishing I could give her the one little piece of information that could take away her pain, yet knowing I'm not supposed to say anything, for Jay's sake. *If you'd done your job as a boyfriend, Brother Dear, I wouldn't be in the middle of this mess. . . .*

"Hey, sorry about all this," Val says, smiling awkwardly through her tears. "You're his sister—

it's not fair to get you involved. It's just that you two are so close—I thought you might know something."

It's funny how Jay claims to be an authority on everything, and yet when it comes to simple communication with his girlfriend, he doesn't know squat. Maybe it's *my* turn to teach *him*. . . .

"There's something you should know, Val," I start slowly, "but you've got to promise not to tell Jay I told you."

By the time we reach Rockfish Gap, where the Blue Ridge Parkway meets Skyline Drive, the secret is burning brightly between us, forming a bond so electric, you'd think we were sisters already. Val's somber mood has transformed into a giddy playfulness, occasionally punctuated by a sudden burst of disbelieving, joyful laughter. She's completely blown away that Jay is planning a marriage proposal. I'm so happy to be the one to turn her around, yet I can't seem to push aside the persistent feeling that I've made a dumb mistake. It's not that I'm afraid Val will tell Jay about our conversation; it's that I'm thinking I might've taken some of the steam out of Jay's big moment.

On the other hand, if I had let Val continue being frustrated with Jay, that big moment might never happen. And that would definitely be much worse than me spilling a little privileged information. Wouldn't it?

At the southern gate of Shenandoah National Park, Val flashes her season pass to one of the park rangers, and we continue the graceful climb up the crest, behind a steady line of RVs and family-packed minivans. Thankfully, the speed limit at Skyline Drive drops to thirty-five miles per hour, keeping Val's lead foot in check. Considering the ecstatic mood she's in, I wouldn't be surprised if she tried to break the sound barrier.

My ears continue to pop as we ascend the winding road. "I'm so psyched! I totally wanted to come here."

"I know." Val beams. "Jay told me."

I smile. "Even though he can be a pain, he's a really good guy."

"Yeah, he is," she answers, bobbing in her seat, practically ready to burst.

"I need to find myself a guy," I muse, staring dreamily out the window. "Do you know any good guys?"

"What about that one?" she answers, pointing to a cyclist with a killer bod up ahead, dressed in blue and yellow gear. "He looks pretty good."

"Mmmm-hmmm," I hum. Maybe it's the higher altitude or a bout of temporary insanity, but the next thing I know, I'm sticking my head out the window, blowing the cyclist a string of air kisses.

"What are you doing?" Val shrieks with laughter.

"Marry me!" I shout into the wind. He looks over his shoulder, muscular legs pumping against the steep grade, and gives me a cool wave as we ride by.

"I'll pull over so you two can get to know one another better," Val teases, letting her foot off the gas.

"Are you crazy?" I shrill, watching the cyclist draw closer in the side mirror. My carefree laughter suddenly takes on a panicked edge. "Keep going!"

Val hangs back one second longer, just to torment me, then stomps her foot to the floor. The cyclist slips back, quickly becoming a distant blur of blue and yellow.

A patchwork of gold sunlight falls across the two-lane road, filtered through the dense growth of trees hugging both sides of the drive. The road curves and climbs, revealing only one small stretch at a time and a canopy of deep blue sky up ahead. With leafy branches sheltering us on either side, it seems as though we are hardly elevated at all, until a sharp corner and an opening in the tree line bring the mountainside into full view. The air catches in my throat as I gaze with awe down the eastern slope of the Blue Ridge, its foothills smoothing out gently into a lush bed of rich farmland.

"That's called the Piedmont," Val says. "Farm country. It runs right through the middle of Virginia."

"Can we stop and take a look?" I say, struggling to take in the view from the confines of Val's sports car. There's a scenic overlook only a few feet ahead, where several visitors have parked to stretch their legs and take pictures.

"Let's wait—there are better things to see." Val doesn't even look back as we roll past the turnoff and the tourists staring solemnly at the panoramic view. I can't even imagine what it's like to be able to take such amazing natural beauty for granted.

"You've been here a lot?"

"Millions of times," Val says. "I usually try to avoid it in the summer, though. With all the tourists, traffic can be horrendous."

Every new curve of the road brings with it a new vista, a new wonder, a new opportunity to soak up nature, all of which I've been trying to take in at a steady thirty-five miles per hour. My arms and legs feel like loaded coils, ready to spring free from the moving car and tour the park at a reasonable pace. Instead of diving out at the next overlook, though, I decide to stick it out awhile longer, have a little faith that my future sister-in-law will eventually come through for me.

And twenty minutes later, she does. Big time.

Instead of pulling off at one of the popular stops, Val parks the car in a small, shady pocket and tells me to follow her across to the other side of the road. The air is definitely cooler than it was in Waynesboro, about ten degrees' difference, I think, but the sun is warm. Dodging an RV with four bikes on top of it, I bound across the road and trail Val as she swerves through a maze of shrubs and low bushes.

"Do you have something against trails?" I joke,

holding my breath as a prickly bush grazes my bare calf. *Does she know where she's going, or is she just winging it?* I wonder silently as I block my face from the snapping branches Val leaves in her wake. I hope she's not too busy thinking about what I'd said to pay attention to where she's going. All it takes is a split-second thought about bridal gowns and Val could end up leading us right into the clutches of an overprotective mother bear and her two baby cubs. Or maybe she could lapse into a daydream about the bouquet toss. I can see it now—she'll fling her arms into the air, lose her balance, and go sailing right off the edge of a cliff. I'll tell you right now, I'm not going after *that* bouquet.

"It's not far," Val calls back to me. "I want you to get a good view."

Moments later we come to a clearing, and instantly I realize Val was right. It was worth the trouble.

"It's so majestic," I whisper, though no one else is around. Looking out to the west of the ridge, the Shenandoah Valley spreads out before us in all its splendor, a sweeping expanse of earth and sky that just go on forever. Directly below us, the treetops make a soft green velvet staircase down to the bottom of the valley, where tiny houses fleck the landscape. Through the veil of the white-gray mist that hangs over the valley interior, I can make out the vague backbone of another chain of mountains.

"Are those part of the Blue Ridge?" I ask.

"No, those are the Allegheny Mountains," Val says, leaning back against a boulder. "Together with the Blue Ridge, they make up the Shenandoah Valley."

I nod slowly. "I can't believe how foggy it is up here."

"It's not fog—it's pollution," she says with a sad tinge to her voice. "It's actually not too bad today."

My jaw drops. "But how? I haven't seen *that* much industry around here."

"It comes from the Midwest, supposedly. Like around Ohio and Indiana. It wasn't always like this, though—I remember the air being pretty clear when I was younger."

I turn around and start heading back to the road, and Val follows me without saying a word. I wish I could stay and take in what's left of the view, but I can't. It's just too depressing.

At milepost 51.2, we stop at one of the more popular attractions in the park—a little piece of paradise called Big Meadows. That's exactly what it is, too—a huge, open, bowl-shaped meadow that the park map says covers about 150 acres. It also says that the ground tends to be swampy in this area most of the year, which I can tell you firsthand is true—already I can feel some of the dampness seeping into the soles of my shoes.

Big Meadows is nothing less than inspiring. While there's a lot to do around here—horseback riding, hiking, restaurants—Val and I are pretty content to grab a spot at one of the picnic tables and just take in the view. The meadow is blanketed with tender green ferns and tons of delicate wildflowers. I don't know the names of many of the flowers, but I do recognize the puffy petals of a yellow lady's slipper nearby. My favorite flowers, though, are the fist-sized clusters of bluish-purple petals hiding among the tall grasses, each with its own collar of leaves. I've never seen anything like it.

"Check it out—" Val nudges me in the direction of a puddle a few yards away, where a white-tailed doe and her two fawns have paused to take a drink. I hold my breath, afraid that the slightest movement will scare the deer away, spoiling the serene moment.

Val and I smile as we watch the youngest one, with her knobby knees and stick legs, leaning precariously over the water. Just then, a man at the picnic table next to us whips out his video camera and starts taping everything, crouching in the grass and creeping up to the poor animals like he's about to ambush them.

Sometimes I really hate people. Especially when they act like tourists.

"Why doesn't he leave them alone?" I groan under my breath, watching the man snake closer to the deer. You'd think the mother would be startled at the sight of a pudgy man with a video camera practically crawling on his belly to get her and her babies on tape, but she just keeps on drinking, ignoring him the whole time.

"The deer are so used to people around here, they're practically tame," Val explains. "It's almost like a petting zoo sometimes."

If there was a way to keep all the people away, I think this would be the perfect place to live. I can see myself trying the Henry David Thoreau thing—camping out in the wilderness for a few years of perfect solitude and reflection, communing with nature, and visiting civilization only once in a while so I don't completely lose my mind out here in the mountains. There's always been something really appealing to me about living alone in an isolated area, learning every detail of the surrounding land. There's so much to see if you just stop and take the time to look really closely. I think I could be happy settling down in one spot, knowing all there is to know about my tiny corner of the world.

On the other hand, there's a part of me that has this need to cover as much ground as possible, to get a little taste of everything that's out there. When I was eight or so, I remember being in the dentist's waiting room, pacing the floor while Mom read magazines. To onlookers, it might've seemed that I was walking around aimlessly, but in reality my footsteps were part of a very precise game I'd invented for myself where I tried to cover every square inch of the floor with the soles of my white and blue sneakers. I felt like a pioneer of sorts— each tile I touched became claimed territory. I wanted my invisible footprints to be everywhere.

And the waiting room was only the beginning. I had visions of covering the parking lot, too, and the sidewalk, and the lawn out front, and the road leading back to our house. When I'd covered all of Greenwich, I'd go to Stamford and Darien; when I'd covered all of Connecticut, I'd work on the rest of New England. At that time, I saw myself eventually covering every single inch of the United States—maybe even the whole world.

Now I know it would be physically impossible to walk the entire Earth, but much of that pioneer spirit remains. Still, I can't decide if it's better to know a little about every place, or to know everything about a little place.

"Hey, check this out," I say, pointing out our location on the map. "We're right near Dark Hollow Falls. Is it nice?"

Val shrugs. "I guess, if you're into waterfalls."

Who isn't? I wonder to myself. "Can we go?"

"It'll probably take forever to get down there," she says, drumming her long pink nails against the top of the picnic table.

I consult the map again. "The trail is just a little over half a mile. It's not far at all," I say, giving her a pleading look.

"All right," Val answers, pursing her lips. "Let's check it out."

My pulse quickens in anticipation as we pick up the start of the trail at the campground nearby. We make it to the falls in almost no time at all, mostly because Val runs the whole way, sandaled feet kicking up dust behind her while I trail breathlessly behind. So much for appreciating nature. It's obvious Val's interest in being a tour guide is rapidly dropping. As much as I enjoy her company, it would be nice if I could be out here on my own to take things at a slower pace.

"This is it," Val says when we reach the edge of the falls, sounding uninspired. The powerful cascade of water rushing over smooth black rocks fills the air with white noise. Tiny droplets of water land on my arm, making me thirst for a swim in the foam. Out of the corner of my eye I notice Val fidgeting. We just got here, and she looks like she wants to leave already.

"I guess I didn't need my sweater after all," I say, stalling for time. "It's pretty warm, even down here."

"The sweater was for another place I had in mind."

"Oh?"

Val nods. "But maybe I planned too much for one day, though. If you want to spend the rest of the afternoon here, we can skip it."

The spark of Val's suggestions leaves me burning with curiosity. "I think I've seen enough," I say, retracing my footsteps. "Race you back to the parking lot!"

At the nearest park exit we're zooming on the highway again, heading west, then north for what seems like hours. Val won't give in, no matter how hard I try to pump her for clues.

"An ice-skating rink."

"Excuse me?" Val asks.

"You're taking me to an indoor ice-skating rink, right?"

"Nope. Not even close."

"Then what about a boat ride?" I say, closely watching her reaction. "It can get pretty cold on the water."

Val snickers. "We're in the mountains, Miranda."

"So? What are you trying to say?" I laugh, totally stumped. "Don't worry—I'll figure it out before we get there. It's tough to surprise me."

We take the next exit at a town called Luray. "Time's almost up," Val announces. "Any last-minute guesses?"

Just when I'm about to give up, I spot a sign in

the distance for LURAY CAVERNS. Of course—it makes perfect sense.

"Wait a minute . . . it's coming to me. . . . " I close my eyes and rub my forehead as if I'm receiving psychic waves from the atmosphere. "Is it Luray Caverns?"

"No fair. You saw the sign."

"What sign?" I ask with an innocent smile.

I've seen caverns on TV many times and read about them in books, but I've never had the opportunity to see them in person, so I'm totally psyched to be here. After buying our tickets, Shannon, the tour guide, leads our group of fifteen people down into the caverns, where the temperature of the air feels like it's instantly dropped about thirty degrees. It's dark down here, except for the colored spotlights that highlight sharp, rocky spikes hanging from the ceiling and jutting from the floor like shark's teeth. The enormous underground chamber is alien and unreal—like the landscape of Mars or what you'd imagine the underworld to look like.

"Kind of gives you chills, doesn't it?" Val whispers.

Shannon explains that what we're looking at is what she likes to think of as the skeleton of the Blue Ridge Mountains. She says that most of the hills in this area have underground caverns, created by the slow drip of rainfall as it seeps deep into the soil, picking up acids and eventually eating away at the limestone underneath—a process that has taken over 400 million years. What is left behind is the gigantic hollowed-out pocket we're standing in right now.

"Does anyone know the difference between a stalactite and a stalagmite?" Shannon asks, folding her arms primly behind her back.

An eleven-year-old boy in the front row of our group raises his hand. "A stalactite hangs from the ceiling," he answers smugly as he points to one of the icicle-shaped mineral formations above our heads. "And a stalagmite comes from the floor up."

"Very good," Shannon says in a perky voice. "A good way to remember the difference is to think that a stalac*tite* has to hold on *tight* to keep from falling."

"I don't need tricks to remember things," the kid says smugly. "I have a photographic memory."

One of the most amazing stops on our tour is at Dream Lake, a pool of water so still that it creates a perfect reflection of the ceiling above, giving the illusion that you're staring down at a chasm thousands of feet deep. I'm shocked when Shannon tells us the water is only two feet deep. Beyond that is a gigantic column called Pluto's Ghost, which was made when a stalactite and a stalagmite fused together, growing into one large mass over the years. Even deeper into the cavern, we come across a shimmering white formation of calcite, which has spread out like a frozen version of Dark Hollow Falls. It's called Titania's Veil, which I recognize as being named after the Queen of the Fairies in Shakespeare's play *A Midsummer Night's Dream.* If I remember right, Titania, along with Oberon, the King of the Fairies, had the power to bless marriages between humans. Judging by the serene way Val is gazing at the waterfall-shaped calcite, I'd guess she made the same connection. The tour group moves on, but we stay put.

"Are you sure Jay wants to marry me?" Val asks. In the strange acoustics of the cavern, her soft voice seems to be coming at me from all sides.

"I know my brother," I answer, leaning against the metal railing. "He couldn't be more serious about you."

An ecstatic little gasp escapes from Val's throat. "I just can't believe it—we're only halfway through school. I've thought about what it would be like marrying Jay, of course, but I never dreamed it would be so soon."

"Hang on a second—" I interrupt. "We don't have any idea how soon it will be . . . he might even wait until you're almost ready to graduate before he pops the question. I just wanted you to know that he's thinking about you in a long-term way and that you have no reason to feel insecure about your relationship."

"Right . . . " Val exhales and seems to float back to Earth for a moment or two before soaring up into the clouds again. "Do you think Jay would want to get married here, in Virginia? I know this beautiful spot where the ceremony could take place. I've always wanted to get married outdoors."

Val's usually so cool about everything that I'm really surprised at how crazy she's acting. It's making me just a tad nervous. "I know this is really exciting for you, but please don't get carried away. It could still be a long way off."

"Right . . . ," she says with a faraway look in her eyes that tells me I'm still not getting through.

We rejoin the group just as Shannon is talking about the cavern's famous Stalacpipe Organ, an organ built by a man named Leland Sprinkle over forty years ago. It works in much the same way that a pipe organ works, except it uses thirty-seven stalactites instead of pipes to make its sound.

"We call this part of the cavern The Cathedral," Shannon says, leading us into a circular chamber. "In fact, many wedding ceremonies have taken place here."

Val giggles and nudges my elbow. "Do you think Jay would want to get married down in here?"

Picturing my straitlaced brother in a tux, getting married in a musty underground cave is just too funny. "No way," I answer, our laughter echoing off the jagged walls.

Val is still riding high on her wedding rush, unable to talk about anything but wedding gowns for the entire ride back to Waynesboro. My head is swimming in tulle, chapel-length trains, and three-tiered veils. Val already knows every little detail of her wedding, right down to the color of the table linens, as if she's been planning for this since the age of five. The bridesmaids' dresses she has in mind sound gorgeous—I can't wait to try on mine.

By the time we reach Jay's apartment, we're both whipped up into a matrimonial frenzy. This scares me a little because I'm afraid that if Val comes inside the apartment with me, one of us will slip up and accidentally mention the wedding in front of Jay.

I hate keeping secrets. They're so much *work*.

"Do you want to come in?" I ask just to be polite.

Thankfully, Val shakes her head. "I want to get to the bookstore before it closes to see if they have any wedding planners."

I'm so excited for her, but my heart dies a little.

"Please don't get too carried away, Val. Remember, I wasn't supposed to tell you—"

"I know," Val says, getting serious. "Don't worry—I won't say anything to Jay. I'm just having a little fun, that's all."

"Okay," I answer with a relieved smile. "Thanks a lot for today. I had a great time."

"Me, too. It's kind of nice having a sister."

"I know," I say. "I already have one, but I know what you mean. It'd be great to have you in the family, Val."

Val smiles. "Give Jay my love."

"I will."

The car door barely shuts behind me before Val peals out of the driveway at breakneck speed. I walk up the path with tired legs and find Darren sitting on the front steps, battling with the plastic buckles on a shiny new pair of in-line skates.

Oh, no.

"So, what do you think of my new wheels?" he says, lifting one lumbering foot into the air. "I just got 'em tonight."

"They're slick," I say, noting with dread the lightning bolts on either side of the boot. "They look fast."

"Top of the line. These babies are the kind of skate they use in competitions." Darren grunts as he snaps the top buckle closed, nearly catching the skin of his index finger in the process. "I got them on clearance."

"How long have you been skating?"

Darren smiles proudly. "This is my first time. I've never been on skates *ever.*"

That's exactly what I was afraid of. A cold shiver runs through my body. Darren just might make a house builder out of me yet. "You should really think about getting some pads before you go out there," I say, noticing his bare, knobby knees and elbows. "You might break something."

"Nah—I'll be fine." Darren lets go of the railing and tries to take a step forward but gets freaked out by the sensation and throws his weight backwards. I duck just before one of his long, floppy arms has the chance to whack me across the cheek, and look up expecting to see him knocked out cold on the pavement. Instead, Darren is bending and thrashing in all directions, locked in the ultimate struggle with the laws of physics. To make matters even worse, the wheels of his skates have begun their smooth descent down the slope of the driveway, gathering an impressive rate of speed. Impressive, that is, if you're a competitor. Totally terrifying if you're Darren.

"Lean hard on the back of your right skate to stop!" I shout as he takes off down the street, his high-pitched cries of fright piercing the night air. I wince thinking about the hill waiting for him below. It's a long way down.

"Hey, there—" Jay says when I walk in. He's sitting at the kitchen table taking notes from a college economics textbook. Most people think of summer as vacation time. Jay sees it as one big study hall.

"Keep your ears open," I say, closing the screen door. "If you hear an ambulance, it's probably your roommate."

Jay chuckles. "You saw the skates."

"He's rolling down the hill as we speak, speeding toward his doom." I kick off my sandals and leave them right where they fall.

"So how was your day? Did you have fun?" Jay says, highlighting a paragraph in fluorescent orange.

Slumping tiredly into a kitchen chair, I let my arms dangle lazily on either side of me. "It was great. We went up Skyline Drive, checked out a few places in the park, went to Luray Caverns . . . "

And, oh yeah . . . I almost forgot . . . I sort of proposed to your girlfriend for you.

"Did she leave?" he says, craning his neck to look out the window.

"Yeah." I swear I can feel my internal organs shriveling like prunes. "She said she wanted to get to the bookstore before it closed."

Val's probably tearing up and down the aisles right now, yanking every wedding book and bridal magazine ever published off the shelves, much to the dismay of the bookstore employees who were hoping to get home at a decent hour. *Yes, I'll have one of each, please. No, no . . . my boyfriend hasn't proposed yet. I just want to be prepared when he does.*

Jay's brow furrows curiously for a moment, then relaxes. "So you had a good time?"

I nod maturely. "It was an enlightening and educational experience." Out of the corner of my eye, I can see my brother doing a double take. "When I was sitting up there today, looking over the valley, seeing the whole world below me, I asked myself, *What do you want out of life? Where do you see yourself ten years from now?*"

Jay leans forward on his elbows. "And what did you come up with?"

"Not a darn thing," I say with a smile.

"Join the club," my brother says with a sigh. "The older I get, the more unsure I am about everything."

"Come on, Jay," I scoff. "You're going to school, you've got a great career ahead of you, and you've got Val—what's there to be unsure about?"

A strange, vacant look comes to my brother's eyes. "Nothing."

Sunscreen . . . *lawn chair . . . iced tea . . . darn, I forgot the iced tea. . . .*

Hopping barefooted across the hot tar driveway to the screen door, I find my tall glass of tea still sitting on the counter, right where I'd left it. I take a long, cold drink and head back out again to the sunshine, where a rusty old lawn chair is waiting for me in the backyard, adjusted to the perfect angle for maximum comfort. My only ambition this afternoon is to be as lazy as humanly possible.

It's good to have goals, isn't it?

Sitting here like this, with the warmth of the sun sinking deep into my bones, reminds me of summer days when Chloe and I were in elementary school. One of our favorite pastimes was to set up my collection of Barbie dolls in various poses on our picnic table, then blast them away with my mom's garden hose. It was kind of like one of those carnival games, except we always won. If you hit her just right, Barbie sure could fly. Mom must've thought we were nuts. Chloe claims we were merely expressing our frustration with the lack of progress in feminism. I think we were just two bored kids, looking for some harmless fun. Thinking back now, though, I'm wondering if maybe Chloe was right. Any psychologist who had watched us collect the dripping wet Barbies and hang them by their hair on the clothesline to dry when we were done would have probably thought we had some serious issues.

I feel like reading something . . . I need a book. . . .

Bouncing off the chair (for what I hope will be the last time), I go back into the apartment to find something to read. I scour the living room, but there isn't too much around aside from Jay's economics books and scraps of old newspapers. Darren doesn't seem to be much of a reader—he's too busy trying to find ways to hurt himself. By the way, he managed to return from skating last night in one piece, telling us how he miraculously cheated death by covering his eyes when he was heading straight for a stalled pickup truck. By the time he reached the bottom of the hill, Darren opened his eyes to find the truck gone. He said it was so much fun, he went all over town like that, never figuring out how to stop and just covering his eyes when something got in his way. And he claims he never fell—not even once.

I made Darren swear he'll buy a helmet and pads tonight, but I'm afraid it won't be enough. I'm thinking he'll need something more along the lines of body armor, just to be on the safe side. Maybe we can rig something up with pillows, blankets, and a little bit of rope.

Okay . . . I've narrowed my reading choices down to two books: Jay's economics textbook and the phone book. Both appear to be equally entertaining, but the economics book wins out because it has better pictures. The most I can hope for at this point is that it'll put me to sleep quickly.

Just when I settle back in my lawn chair and start learning about the law of diminishing returns, the phone rings.

"What now?" I groan, going back into the apartment for the umpteenth time. I suppose I should just let the machine pick up the call, but something tells me in my gut to answer it. "Hello?"

"I'm so glad you're home," Jay says, sounding breathless.

"I was afraid it was you," I answer. "Don't worry—the cops just busted up the party. Other than the fire on the living room rug, there wasn't that much damage, considering—"

Instead of playing along, Jay cuts right to the chase. "I need to ask you a favor."

"Oh, no . . . "

"Leann needs to go to class in an hour, and her baby-sitter just quit."

"The woman whose house you're building?" I ask.

"Yeah. She's frantic. Can you do it?"

A fuzzy feeling of dread crawls up my throat. "*If* I were to do it, what would I have to do?"

"I don't know," Jay says. "Just watch her son for a couple of hours."

"How old is he?"

"Almost two, I think. It'd be just for today."

"I have no way of getting there," I answer, twisting the phone cord around my fingers.

"I left you my car for the day," he counters. "Remember?"

"How come someone from the crew doesn't volunteer?" I ask.

"We're setting the main beam right now and attaching the floor joists."

"Huh?"

"We're on a tight schedule and need all the hands we can get." Jay exhales loudly in my ear. "We don't have a lot of time here, M. Can you do it or not?"

A deep groan ripples up from my toes and goes through every part of my body as I think of my relaxing afternoon going to waste. Life is so unfair. I suddenly think of the promise I'd made to myself to act more like an adult around Jay, and realize that by not doing this favor I could lose a lot of ground with him.

"All right." I sigh. "I'll do it."

This can't be it," I say out loud to myself, double-checking the directions Jay gave me three times. *"Coral Gable Estates,"* he said. Not only is this place missing both gables and coral, it doesn't resemble anything remotely close to an estate. If it wasn't for the small, peeling sign hanging above the doorway of the gray-shingled apartment building, I never would've known this was it.

You could always say you didn't find it, a devious voice whispers in my head. *It would be so easy to turn around and go back. No one would ever know. . . .*

"But *I'd* know," I tell myself, pulling Jay's car into a parking space next to an old, dented car with a broken trunk lock. Life would be so much easier if I didn't have a conscience that kept getting in the way of things.

A group of five guys around my age are hanging out by the front entrance to the building. They aren't really doing anything, but I'm getting a weird vibe like they might be up to something or they're at least thinking about it. I lock the car door and start up the dirt path with my eyes glued to the ground and my stomach churning sourly. Having to walk by a group of guys alone is one of the things I hate most about being a girl.

Apartment 2B . . . apartment 2B . . . , I repeat the words in my head like a chant to drown out the comments being hurled at me.

"Hey, baby . . . ," one of them calls. "I'm talking to you. What's the matter? You don't talk?"

Another one whistles. "She's all right. I'd go for some of that."

"You know what they say about redheads. . . . "

I hear whispering, then loud snickering behind me. When I get to the door, I frantically hit the buzzer for apartment 2B, feeling a rush of hot blood rising to the surface of my skin.

Open up . . . please . . . I try to look as tough as steel, but inside I'm wilting. *Jay, you are going to pay for this.*

"Nobody's in there," one of the guys says with a laugh. "But if you come over here, I'll keep you company."

I almost believe him, but then the door buzzer sounds and I quickly slip into the building, slamming the door behind me. I wish I could think of some cutting remark to sling back at those guys, but I figure they're not worth the effort.

"Sorry I couldn't get to the door sooner," a woman's voice calls from the top of the dark

101

staircase. "Noah just knocked over one of my plants and . . . well, it's just been a crazy day."

Following the voice, I ascend the creaky stairs, my hand grazing along the broken plaster wall to guide my way through the dank hall. Exposed wires hang from the ceiling where a light fixture might've been once. Murky brown water stains bleed from the ceiling. The air is stale and acrid, with dust particles dancing in the thin gray sunbeam filtering through a dirty window. I hate to say it, but this place is a real dump.

"Thanks for coming on such short notice. Jay's said so many great things about you," the woman says. Her voice sounds careworn, yet hopeful—the voice of an overworked mother. Against the dim light of the window, I can only see the outline of the woman's slight build and limp, shoulder-length hair.

"I suppose he has to say nice things—he's my brother," I say lightly, trying not to seem too jarred by the surroundings and the situation. It's hard to believe that less than an hour ago I was dozing happily on a lawn chair, with the whole afternoon to myself. I feel strung out already.

"I'm sure Jay wouldn't have said that if he didn't mean it," she says. "By the way, I'm Leann."

As I reach the top step, Leann's weary features fill in—drawn cheeks, bleary eyes, cautiously optimistic smile. She's only about half my size in height and bone structure, yet the strength of her presence would make you think of someone much larger in stature.

"Come on in . . . please excuse the mess," she says, ducking into the apartment with me following behind apprehensively.

The apartment is brighter than the hallway, though not by much. Old, rusty appliances fill the tiny kitchen, leaving just enough room for a small table and two chairs. On the gray floor is an overturned terra-cotta pot and a pile of black potting soil strewn all over the place, and in the middle of all of this, clutching the roots of the plant in his pudgy little fist, is the cutest little boy I think I've ever seen.

"Pant," he says.

"Right, that's a plant," Leann answers patiently. She scoops up her son and balances him on the edge of the sink, washing his grimy fingers under running water. "Noah's at that stage where he's into everything. You really have to keep an eye on him."

I'm still standing by the door, feeling totally useless. "Do you need any help?"

"Would you mind sweeping up? There's a broom hanging behind the bathroom door."

"Sure."

While I sweep, Leann brushes the lint off her clothes and gives Noah a bear hug and a kiss on the tip of his nose. "Mommy has to go to school now, but Miranda's going to stay with you. You be

103

a good boy, okay?" She grabs her purse and keys. "The number's on the fridge. I'm going to stop and pick up a few groceries on the way home, so I'll be back around six-thirty. If Noah gets hungry, you can make him a snack."

"Okay."

"Make sure to lock the door behind me, and if anyone knocks, don't answer."

"Okay." Now I'm *really* getting creeped out by this place.

"Bye, sweetie," Leann says, blowing Noah a kiss. "See you soon."

The door closes, and Noah looks up at me with his big blue eyes, as if he's trying to make sense of everything going on. He then looks back at the place where his mother was standing, then back to me again, and when he seems to have the situation straight in his head, he smiles and sticks his hands right back into the pile of dirt.

I'm trying my best not to seem panicked, but beads of sweat are forming along my temples and are trickling down the sides of my face.

"Noah, please give me the quarter," I say calmly.

Noah gives me a tight-lipped smile and shakes his head.

"If you give me the quarter, I'll make you a snack. Would you like that?"

He shakes his head again.

I reach for the kid, but he jerks away suddenly, which totally scares me. One wrong move and this could turn into a disaster. I feel like a negotiator trying to talk someone out of jumping off a sky-scraper ledge.

"I know where there is this huge candy machine that you can put a quarter into and it gives you lots of candy. If you give me the quarter, I'll show you where it is."

All right, so what if I'm resorting to blatant

lies. I'll deal with the consequences later. This is a serious situation: As long as he does what I want, I don't care.

Noah stares at me stubbornly.

"Okay, that's it," I say, hardening my voice. I cup my hand under his chin. "No more negotiating, Noah. Give me the quarter."

For one terrifying second, I'm afraid he's going to tilt his head back, but then his mouth opens, and the slimy silver coin comes tumbling out into my hand. My body goes slack with relief.

Six minutes down, 174 more to go.

"How about I read you a story?" I say, picking up Noah and setting him beside me on the couch. I grab the nearest picture book—something about puppies and kittens—but before I even crack it open, Noah wriggles off the couch and tries to stick one of his chubby little fingers in an electrical outlet. I dive for him like a baseball player sliding into home, my heart nearly popping out of my chest.

"Don't do that," I say as firmly as I can without scaring Noah. He gives me a sidelong glance with his big blue eyes, like he knows exactly what he's doing, then struts off toward the bedroom to see what else he can get away with now that his mother's not here. It's hard to believe this adorable little person could be such a challenge to take care of, but here I am running around like an idiot trying to keep him from destroying the apartment. If he's not uprooting plants and trying to electrocute himself, he's playing in the toilet or eating garbage. And every time I hold him, he wiggles out of my grasp like a slippery little worm.

If this is what having kids is like, I'm going to have to seriously reconsider, I tell myself as I wrestle a sharp pencil from Noah's iron grip. Parenting isn't supposed to be easy, but a person could go nuts chasing little ones around the house every second of the day, keeping them out of trouble. Their one redeeming quality, though, is that they're so darn cute. If it wasn't for that, I'm sure the human race would've ended centuries ago.

Just kidding . . .

The truth is, I really look forward to having kids of my own someday, but only when the circumstances are exactly right. First, I want to be all settled into my career and happily married and have gotten everything I want to do out of the way, so I can devote my full attention and energy to motherhood. I'm not like Leann, who can handle school, a job, and raising a kid all at once.

"I wannack," Noah says, yanking a fistful of my hair and looking terribly serious.

"What, Noah?" I answer patiently as tears of pain come to my eyes.

"Nack," he says with a tug.

"Snack? You want a snack?"

He nods.

Now we're getting somewhere.

I like to think of myself as an optimist, as someone who looks for the bright side of things, which is why I'm trying to find some artistic integrity in a design most people would immediately dismiss with irritation.

THE ARTIST: *noah*
THE CANVAS: *the kitchen*
THE MEDIUM: *peanut butter on a cracker*

"Nice, bold strokes," I say, squinting and rubbing my chin. "You've obviously been influenced heavily by the likes of Kline and de Kooning, and the way the peanut butter fades from light to dark on the oven door reminds me of Mark Rothko."

"Door," the artist gurgles.

I won't even *try* to explain how Noah managed to remodel the kitchen and himself while my back was turned for only two seconds, but let's just say he's passionate about his art.

"Into the bath you go," I say, carrying the sticky,

squirming, peanut-smelling toddler to the tub, clothes and all. The minute I start running the warm water, Noah kicks and squeals, his peanut butter arms whacking me—I mean, he's going nuts. I squirt some soap on a big sponge and lather him up, but none of the stuff wants to come off.

This sucks.

I never should've let Jay guilt me into doing this. . . . I never should've answered the stupid phone when I heard it ring. . . . I could be dozing in the backyard right now. . . . I never should've even come to Virginia. . . . This whole thing's been a colossal waste of time. . . .

"Go . . . down . . . the . . . drain!" I shout impatiently, plunging the bathtub drain that's now clogged with peanut butter. Noah, who's sitting on the bathroom rug wrapped in a towel, is staring at me, looking severely traumatized and shivering. My anger melts away in an instant, and my heart is suddenly filled with aching remorse. "It's okay, little guy," I say, picking Noah up and giving him a hug, "everything's okay."

I abandon the tub for the moment to bring Noah to the bedroom to change him into some dry clothes, to swap his now sopping wet diaper for a new one (should've thought of that *before* I put him in the tub!), and to gently towel-dry his wet head. Noah's calmed down a lot, though his eyes are red and he keeps sucking in his lower lip like he's going to cry any second. Poor little guy.

It has to be tough for him to have some stranger come into his house and take care of him. I can't help wondering how Noah's daddy fits into all of this, but I get the feeling he's around only some of the time or not at all—Leann wasn't wearing a wedding ring, and the only bed in the apartment besides the baby's is just big enough for one person. I sing to Noah and play peekaboo under the towel until he smiles again.

It takes me forever to scrub the oily residue off the insides of the tub. My arms are aching, and I still haven't done anything about the mess in the kitchen. Noah seems to know it's time to get serious and plays quietly with his bath toys on the floor next to me, occasionally tossing in a rubber duck or a plastic boat. Hopefully, I'll be able to get everything in good shape before Leann gets home.

"Hello?" I hear a voice calling from the kitchen. "Where's my little pumpkin?"

Or maybe not.

A spark lights Noah's eyes at the sound of his mother's voice, and he goes running out into the kitchen, squealing. I tag along behind, feeling slightly embarrassed that Leann is coming home to a war zone.

"Looks like you kept Miranda busy," Leann says, surveying the kitchen. She pulls a toy out of a grocery bag and gives it to him.

"Sorry about the mess," I apologize. "I turned around for two seconds . . . "

"It's all right." Leann gives me a tired smile and starts to put away the groceries. "I'm just glad you were able to sit for me on such short notice. Besides, it doesn't bother me if Noah messes up the place a little—it's not like this is a palace or anything."

I wet a dishcloth and get to work on the cabinets and stove, where the peanut butter has already started to take on the consistency of cement. Leann hesitates when she sees me working, as if she wants to say, *"Don't worry, I'll take care of it,"* but she seems too tired to make an issue of it.

"Are you excited to move into your new house?"

I'm just making idle conversation, but the way Leann's face suddenly takes on this ecstatic glow, you'd think I'd just informed her that I'd inherited a million dollars and was going to give her half.

"I'm counting the seconds," she says to me. "We've been living in this dump for a year and a half now, since Noah's father took off. I just pray we get out of here before someone breaks in or the place burns down."

Somehow, I don't find that hard to believe at all.

Leann opens a can of spaghetti and heats it up on the stove. "Have you been to the site? I haven't been able to get there since the basement was put in."

"I was there two days ago."

"How was it? Did it look good?"

I chisel a gob of dried peanut butter with my fingernail. "I don't know much about housebuilding, but everyone else said it looked great."

Leann looks like she's about to burst with happiness. "I have to try to get down there tomorrow—I still have a lot of hours to put in. Besides, I want to see everything."

I frown. "I can't believe they make you work on your own house. I mean, you already have to work, go to school, and take care of Noah—how in the world do you have any time left over to build a house?"

"I find time—it's all part of the deal. My sister and her husband have put in some hours for me, so that helps," Leann says as she stirs the spaghetti. "I don't mind it at all, because this program is the only way I could ever be able to afford good housing for us, and in a decent neighborhood, too. I just couldn't do it on my own."

"So when it's all done, it's yours?"

"I still have to pay for the house, but with all the donations from businesses and volunteers, the payments are a lot more manageable than your average house," Leann says. She stops moving, and her gaze turns wistful. "I'll tell you right now, the day we move into our new house will be the proudest day of my life. For once I'll be able to say, '*Leann, you've done something right.*'"

Let me make you something to eat," Leann says. "How about a sandwich—do you like peanut butter?" The hilarity of this suggestion quickly dawns on her, and we both bust out laughing. "Wait," she says, looking in the fridge. "What about ham and cheese?"

"It's all right, really. I'm fine." Actually, I'm pretty hungry, but I don't want to take her food—it already seems like they have just enough to scrape by as it is. Noah has finished the last of his spaghetti and is dozing fitfully in his high chair. "I should be going—you've had a long day."

"Are you sure? I have to make one for myself, anyway." Leann pulls two plates down from the cupboard and puts two slices of bread on each. Before I can answer one way or the other, she smears yellow mustard on each slice, working quickly from one plate to the next. There's a rigidness in her movements that suggests there's more to making this sandwich than simply being gracious. I think she needs some company.

"I suppose I could have a bite," I say, timidly taking a seat at the narrow kitchen table, soaking in the strangeness of the situation—my peanut-smelling clothes, the crumbling apartment, dinner with some woman I've never met before. I've moved beyond feeling annoyed. Now, I'm treating this more like an adventure.

"There you are." Leann puts a plate and a cold glass of lemonade in front of me and takes a seat. "This is my favorite time of day . . . when things finally mellow out a little."

I take a bite of the sandwich and settle back into the hard wooden chair. "So what are you taking classes for?"

"My GED—I never finished high school." Leann seems neither proud nor ashamed of this fact—she's just telling it like it is. "I got pregnant with Noah my senior year and had to drop out during the last semester."

That means she's only three years older than me—at the most, I realize with disbelief. I never would've dreamed Leann was so young. I feel like a kid next to her.

"It's great that you're going back," I say meekly, not knowing what else to say.

Leann munches thoughtfully on her sandwich. "At the time, I didn't think dropping out was a big deal. I figured, *I'm a smart person, I don't need a diploma to get along in this world.* I guess that's true to some extent, but then, after a while, you hit a wall. Someone won't hire you for a good job because you didn't graduate. Other people are moving ahead in their lives and you're left in the dust, feeling like less of a person. After you hit enough walls, you decide the only way out is to better yourself and finish school." She takes a long drink from her lemonade. "And I'm not just stopping there. When I get my diploma, I'm going on to college. I want my baby to have a good life."

"And soon you'll have a new house," I say.

The glow returns to Leann's cheeks. "You know what just hit me the other day? We're going to have a backyard! Noah's going to have his own place to run around and play! I can't afford a swing set right away, but I'd like to at least get him one of those little plastic pools to sit in."

"I had one of those when I was a kid," I say. "They're awesome."

"I have all kinds of ideas about how I want to decorate the place. I'm so anxious, I can hardly stand it." Leann spaces out for a few seconds, lost somewhere, I'm sure, in her mental collection of wallpaper patterns and carpet samples. She returns to consciousness almost breathless with excitement. "I'm sorry. I keep yammering on about myself—I've hardly given you a chance to talk."

I shrug. "That's okay. I don't have much to tell."

"Everyone has their stories," Leann says. "Tell me one of yours."

Sometimes when you're talking to someone

who's had a rough time, it's hard to tell them about what's been happening to you, especially if things have been going pretty well by comparison. It almost makes you want to apologize for having it so good. Or even if things haven't been so great, you feel like a big jerk for complaining. It's a no-win situation.

"Well, I grew up in Connecticut . . . ," I start, not sure where to go next. "And I just graduated from high school."

"Good for you," Leann says, sounding genuinely pleased. "Are you going to college in the fall?"

I squirm a little in my seat. "I haven't really decided. I might just travel around for a while. . . . "

Leann smiles and nods attentively like she's happy for me, but I don't know her well enough to know if it's for real or not. If I were her, sitting on the other side of the table right now, listening to some privileged kid talk about how she doesn't know if she feels like going to college or not, I'd be feeling pretty resentful. It's weird. For Leann, college is a matter of survival; but for me, it feels like a prison sentence. My parents have the money, I've already been accepted, and I still don't want to go. Leann must think I'm the most spoiled and ungrateful person in the world.

"I'm trying to figure things out first," I try to explain. "I don't know what I want to do with my life and I don't want to go to school and change my mind a hundred times. I'd like to have that all sorted out before I get there."

"That makes sense," Leann says. "You're young, you don't have any responsibilities right now— you should take all the time you need."

"Yeah, I'm not too good at handling responsibility at the moment," I say with a weak laugh. My bones feel like they're shrinking inside me, and my body is sagging into a childlike blob. "I don't think I could handle things as well as you do."

Leann sighs and leans back in her chair. "You'd be surprised. I bet if it came right down to it, you could handle just about anything."

"I doubt that," I say, wondering secretly to myself if she might be right.

I was wondering where you guys were," I say, playing freeze-frame TV as my brother and Darren finally get back from the work site. "Darren and I are supposed to go looking for pads and a helmet for him tonight."

Jay collapses into a chair, looking as beat as an old pair of sneakers. "He's not going anywhere," he says, mooching a handful of my cheese popcorn.

"Why not?"

"Go take a look," Jay answers, nodding toward the kitchen.

What's he talking about? I give my brother a funny look and bound toward the kitchen. What I see there makes my heart wither in my chest. "Darren! What did you do?" I cry, covering my mouth with my palm.

Darren frowns, his eyes wide with trauma. "I broke my wrist," he says, holding up the cast. It covers his hand and about a quarter of his arm, like a fingerless evening glove. "I need to cover it with a plastic bag so I can take a shower. Can you help me find a bag?"

"Of course," I say gently, looking through the collection in the closet for a bag without holes. "So what happened? Did you get smashed with a hammer? Did a beam fall on you?"

"I was taking a break and this woman named Judy was having trouble opening a bag of chips, so I offered to help her. . . . " Darren's voice breaks. "It's a long story."

"Here's a good one," I say, finding a bag. I slip it over his cast and tie a knot at the top. Never in my life have I met anyone with such a high potential for disaster. I feel so sorry for him. "How's that?"

"Pretty good," Darren answers, examining my work. "God, it's really throbbing. I forgot how much a broken arm hurts."

"You've broken your arm before?"

"Only twice," Darren says. "But both times it was the other arm. I've also had a broken foot, a broken leg, and a broken collarbone."

"Ouch!"

"You're telling me," he answers with a proud smirk. "I've cut myself a bunch of times, too."

"Let's not go there . . . ," I say, wrinkling my nose. "Do you need anything? How about some tea?"

Sniffling a little, Darren looks up at me with his big, puppy-dog eyes. "That would be really nice of you."

I put some water in the kettle. "Go ahead and take your shower and it'll be ready when you're done."

"Okay, thanks," he says, his plastic bag crinkling as he leaves the kitchen. When I hear the water running upstairs, I bound back into the living room.

"Poor guy," I whisper to Jay. "He's a wreck."

"He's all right," Jay answers with a wry smile. "He's milking it so you'll take care of him."

I purse my lips, annoyed at Jay's cynicism. "No way . . . "

"Darren's got a big old crush on you, M."

"Shut up—he does not!" I say, tossing a pillow at him. "We're just friends."

Jay rolls his eyes. "You must be totally blind not to see it," he says. "So how did it go at Leann's?"

"Fine," I answer vaguely, staring at the TV screen, wondering if the stuff he's saying about Darren is really true. "You know, since Darren's going to be out of commission for a while, maybe I could help out again at the site."

Jay's eyebrows arch sharply. "Whoa—what's going on here? I thought you hated working on the house."

"I didn't *hate* it. It just wasn't my favorite thing to do," I answer, my cheeks growing warm. "What's with you? First you practically begged me to go with you to the site, and now you don't want me helping out."

"It's not that I don't want you to help out. . . . ," Jay's voice drifts off. "But if you're going to hang around complaining all day . . . "

I give him an injured look. "I did *not* complain all day."

"I don't know what alternate universe *you're* living in, but in my world, you're what's known as a *major whiner.*" Jay then puts his hands on his hips and tries to imitate me, but it just comes out like a pathetic cross between a talking doll and a squeaky door hinge. "*Jay, it's too hot out here. . . . I don't know where this thing goes. . . . Is it time for lunch yet? . . . I can't carry that by myself. . . . My muscles hurt. . . . Is it time to go yet?*" Needless to say, he doesn't sound a *thing* like me.

"You're so funny, I can't stand it," I say, my words dripping with sarcasm. "I'll tell you what— take me to the site tomorrow and I promise I won't whine even once."

Jay snickers. "I wouldn't want you to pop a blood vessel holding it all in."

"Bet you I can do it," I challenge. "For the whole day."

"A bet, huh?" he says, rubbing his palms together. "And what are we betting?"

"The winner gets to ask the loser for a favor," I answer. "Whatever she chooses."

"Or *he* chooses," Jay corrects me. We shake hands on it. "You're on."

My brother has never been someone who takes bets lightly. It's all part of that competitive DNA Dad passed down to him—a gene from which I've been thankfully spared. Winning doesn't mean that much to me, but losing sure does. And I especially hate losing to Jay because he never lets you forget it. Ever.

Once, when I was about ten, we were raking leaves in the backyard, and Jay divided the yard in half, using two maple trees as markers. He bet me he could rake all the leaves in his half of the yard faster than I could in my half. *Knock yourself out*, I thought to myself, watching him run around like a fool to beat me. Of course Jay "won," and I had to listen to my brother brag about his "victory" day and night until I wanted to tear my hair out. He still brings it up sometimes, if you can believe it.

So why would I voluntarily subject myself to Jay's competitive streak, you ask? Good question. First of all, it's not a problem this time, because I'm going to win. I don't mean that in an obnoxious way; it's just a simple fact. See, on the rare occasion when I whine, it's because I'm unhappy and the situation is beyond my control—like a few days ago when Jay dragged me to the site. This time is totally different, though. I *want* to be there. Before, it was just a boring foundation, but now I can see it's the beginning of a new life for Leann and Noah.

Even though Jay doesn't stand a chance of winning the bet, that doesn't keep him from dipping into his old bag of tricks. It started first thing this morning, when he woke me up half an hour earlier than he was supposed to, knowing that the less sleep I have, the crankier I get, thereby increasing the odds that I'll complain about something. Luckily, I was able to catch on quickly to his antics even in my groggy state, so I just smiled sweetly at my brother and wished him a good morning before going into the bathroom and turning on the shower so he wouldn't hear me cursing at a helpless bar of soap.

Even now, as I'm sitting here in the back seat of the car, forcing myself to radiate my own brand of early morning sunshine, I can tell Jay is up to something.

"Chocolate honey dip," Jay says, handing Darren his doughnut and a napkin. "Don't hurt yourself."

Maneuvering awkwardly with his left hand, Darren takes a huge bite. You've really got to admire the guy's tenacity. It would've been so easy for him to take it easy and veg out on the couch for a few weeks, but instead he still wants to come along and help out in whatever small way he can. Jay and I have made a secret pact to make sure we keep Darren away from anything that might cause him harm, like hammers, saws, and hard-to-open potato chip bags.

"This is soooo good," Darren says through a mouthful. "I love doughnuts."

The shiny glaze makes my mouth water. "Me too," I say rather pointedly as my brother takes his time pouring cream and sugar into his coffee. He's just doing it to aggravate me. "Is there anything for me in that bag?" I ask sweetly.

"They didn't have any more custard-filled," Jay says apologetically. "So I got you plain."

Plain!

I'm seething.

Everybody knows that the only people who like plain doughnuts are old men with no teeth who dunk them in bad coffee until it becomes this mooshy sludge that they can drink down because they can't chew anything. . . .

I will not whine . . . I will not whine . . . I will not whine. . . .

"Thanks, *bro*," I say with a sunny yet borderline hostile voice. "This is not a complaint or anything, but just a point for future reference: You don't have to intentionally aggravate me just so you can win the bet."

"I wasn't *trying* to bug you, M," he answers, licking the cream off his fingers from the beautiful pastry he bought for himself. "Don't tell me you're going to lose over a little thing like a doughnut."

"I'm not going to lose at all," I say heavily, taking a determined bite of my dry doughnut. In a fraction of a second, all the moisture in my mouth has been sucked out. Yummy.

"If I remember correctly, you said the same thing a few years ago about a certain leaf-raking bet," Jay snickers.

Oh, yeah? Well, we'll just see who's laughing at the end of the day, Rake Boy.

Good to see you again, Miranda," Marcy says, wiping the sweat off her forehead with the back of her hand. "Ready to pound some nails?"

"Just point me in the right direction." I fasten the tool belt around my waist, my muscles already twitching in rebellion from the weight.

Marcy checks the black plastic sports watch on her wrist and scans the work site with squinted eyes, her freckled nose wrinkling in thought. "Where's the plywood?" she shouts to anyone in general. "We need some plywood over here."

"It's coming," Gary says, draining the last of his cup of coffee. "Steve and T. J. are unloading them off the truck right now."

"We're just about ready to go," Marcy says. She's all business as she walks around the perimeter of the foundation, taking a close look at corners and joints, running her hand over smooth surfaces. Every once in a while she nods her head silently, and a slight smile touches the corners of her mouth. "Looks really good, doesn't it?"

I follow behind her like a little mouse scurrying to keep up. The top of the foundation is no longer open like it was earlier—now it's covered with an intricate network of beams and supports. As far as I'm concerned, it just looks like a deck with huge gaps between the boards.

"I really don't know what I'm looking at," I confess.

Marcy patiently points out the details. "See that big beam running down the center? That's the main beam. The beams running parallel to it are called girders, which support the interior walls and the roof. The beams running perpendicular are the joists."

I nod, slowly letting all the lingo sink in. "So *that's* what Jay was talking about when he mentioned the joists. I thought he was talking about a tool or something."

While we wait for the plywood, Marcy explains the finer points of foundations, like how the intricate network of beams support each other and the entire structure. She also shows me where the doors and the porch are going to go.

"The subfloor's going down today," Marcy says proudly.

At the risk of sounding like a house-building nerd, I have to say that I'm starting to get a little bit excited. "You *will* show me what to do, right?" I plead as the guys lay the four-by-eight sheets of plywood down over the frame. "I don't know what I'm doing."

"Oh, don't worry—you'll do fine," Marcy says, filling her nail apron.

Darren comes jogging over to us, his dirty blond hair sprouting in all directions, wielding a hammer with his one good hand. "You guys need some help?"

Jay's words about Darren having a crush on me keep circling in my head. I really like Darren, but I just don't think of him, you know, in *that* way.

"Darren, aren't you right-handed?" I ask, sounding a little more stern than usual, just so I don't give him any false hopes. "I don't think it's such a good idea for you to be hammering with your left."

"How hard can it be to hit a nail?" he says, clumsily swinging the hammer in the air. I have a sudden urge to run for cover.

Marcy grabs the hammer from his hand in her take-charge sort of way. "Miranda could use some resin-coated sixpenny nails—why don't you find some for her?"

Darren skulks off, looking dejected.

"Disaster averted," I say, sighing with relief.

"For now . . . , " Marcy replies with a wary grin. She springs up onto the foundation frame with athletic grace and an air of intense purpose. "Let me show you what we're doing."

I try to swing my legs up like Marcy did, but only one knee catches, leaving me no other choice but to roll up onto the platform like a beached whale.

"It's really simple," Marcy says, getting a few nails out of her apron. "All you're doing is nailing the plywood to the floor joists. Like this—" She holds a nail in place with her left hand, giving it a light tap with the hammer so the tip of the nail gets imbedded into the wood. Then, she moves her hand away and hammers it down with three full strokes, until the head of the nail is flush with the plywood.

Even I have to admit that it looks pretty easy.

"See? There's nothing to it," Marcy says, already pounding another nail. "You'll want them spaced about six inches apart."

"Where should I start?"

"You can work on the other end of the sheet so I'll be close by. Here are a few nails to get started on before Darren gets back."

Turning my back to Marcy, I kneel at the opposite end of the plywood, a handful of nails scattered around me. On the other side of the yard, Jay is sawing lumber for the walls, blessedly out of earshot in case a complaint unexpectedly oozes out of me—though I wouldn't put it past him to have a few spies hanging around.

Tap bam-bam-bam. Pause. *Tap bam-bam-bam.* The steady rhythm of Marcy's hammer reverberates through the plywood, vibrating every bone in my body. *Okay, you can do this,* I tell myself. *It's not that hard.* I pick up my first nail and roll it between my fingers, deliberating over where to start. It probably wouldn't make a difference at all where I begin, but every time I press the tip of the nail against the board, I get this uneasy twinge in my gut that makes me move the nail a few inches over.

"Make sure you don't smash your thumb," Marcy calls over her shoulder.

Tap bam-bam-bam. Pause. *Tap bam-bam-bam.*

I just know she's going to finish the sheet before I get even one nail in. How lame would that be?

The tip of my tongue pokes out of the corner of my mouth while I force myself to settle on a spot. *There. This is it. This is where my first nail's going to be. It's too late to change my mind. This is where it's going.* Carefully, I hold the nail in place and, with the gentlest tap, I drive the tip into the board.

Phew. I stop for a second to mop up my forehead and admire my handiwork before I continue with phase two. Not bad for a beginner.

"How's it going?" Marcy asks, probably wondering why she hasn't heard any pounding yet.

"Great," I answer. To emphasize the point, I confidently grab my hammer and smack the head of the nail.

130

Bam . . . Bam . . . Bam . . . Bam . . . Bam.

Gee, I thought it would go in easier than this. . . .

Bam . . . Bam . . . Bam . . . Bam . . . Bam . . .

"Give it a good whack," Marcy says.

BAM! Oh, no . . .

"Uh . . . Marcy, can you come here a sec?"

She spins around. "What happened?"

"I bent it," I moan, staring down at the formerly straight nail with its new ninety-degree angle. What was I thinking? I'm not cut out for this. . . .

Marcy comes over and pulls the nail out for me. "You'll get the hang of it, don't worry."

I pick up another nail and position it over the hole. My pulse quickens as I steady the hammer. I think of Leann and Noah walking around on this floor every day. *What if I screw something up and the floor collapses? What if little Noah falls through the hole and cracks his head on the cement in the basement? They deserve a perfect house. I don't want to ruin it. . . .*

"Here are your nails," Darren says, spilling a pile near my knees. He notices my trembling hands. "Having trouble?"

"No," I answer curtly. "I'm just concentrating. You need to focus to do this sort of work."

"Don't be afraid of it," he says, grabbing for my hammer. "Here—you hold the nail, and I'll pound it in for you—"

I pull away from him—fast. "That's okay . . .

thanks, though. Hey, do you think you can get me an iced tea?"

"Sure," he answers, skulking off again.

Turning my attention back to the nail, I psych myself up and just pound the living daylights out of the thing. No second-guessing, no anxiety—I just go for it.

"Check this out," I tell Marcy, beaming proudly at my accomplishment. The nail is straight this time, its head perfectly flush with the wood. It's a great-looking nail if I do say so myself. "What do you think?"

Marcy surveys my work, her lips in a serious pucker. "Much better than last time, but you completely missed the beam underneath," she says, ripping out my beautiful nail. "Try again."

I am a HAMMERING GODDESS! It took me a while to get the hang of it, but now I've got my own rhythm down, and the nails are sinking through the plywood like a hot knife through butter. One by one, Marcy and I leave a trail of nail heads in our wake and pretty soon we're done with one sheet and then onto the next, and the next, and the next. A few of the less-experienced crew members have joined us, the sounds of our hammers combining with theirs into a complex, multilayered beat. My shoulder's growing sore, but I don't want to stop—it's kind of addictive. The more progress you see, the more you want to work.

"How's it going over here?" Jay asks, bringing Marcy and me each a bottle of water.

"Awesome," I say without thinking twice. The level of enthusiasm in my voice surprises even *me*—earlier in the day, I thought I was going to have to fake it.

"Really?" Jay cocks his eyebrows, like he's not

sure if I'm being sarcastic or not. "Marcy, is my little sister making your life miserable?"

"Not at all," Marcy answers, never missing a beat of her hammer. "In fact, she's doing a great job."

I give my brother a smart-alecky *told-you-so* grin.

"I don't believe it," Jay answers, shaking his head. He doesn't seem worried at all that he's in serious danger of losing our bet—actually, he looks like an embarrassingly proud big brother.

"That's my M," he says, tousling my hair affectionately.

I cringe. "Shouldn't you be busy building something?"

Jay takes a drink from his water bottle. "I'm on break."

Picking up the hammer to resume my work, I notice right away that the rhythm is lost. Even as I focus all of my attention on the task at hand, I'm acutely aware of Jay's eyes bearing down on me, ready to pounce with a suggestion, a comment, a critique. Already, my good mood is beginning to fade.

"Maybe you should check on Darren," I suggest. "He mentioned a little while ago that he wanted to see how well he could handle power tools with his one good hand."

"I just saw him," Jay answers coolly. "He was sleeping under a tree."

"Were both arms and legs still attached?"

"What?"

"Did you bother to check to see if he had both of his arms and legs?" I ask gravely. "You assumed he was sleeping, but for all we know, he could be passed out, bleeding to death from a tragic mishap with a table saw."

Marcy snickers.

"Drama Queen," Jay mutters with a wry smile. "I guess you're trying to tell me in your own special way that you don't want me hanging around you while you're working."

I rearrange my nails into a neat line. "Hey— that's not a bad idea."

"All you have to do is say so." Sounding a little miffed, Jay walks off.

Why can't I be straightforward sometimes? I wonder to myself, feeling like a jerk. *Why can't I just say what's on my mind instead of acting like a weirdo?*

Out of the corner of my eye I see the hazy outline of a white T-shirt and blue jeans coming toward me. "Can I help out over here?" a voice says.

I smile when I realize it's Leann. In the bright summer sun she looks healthy and energetic, and the high ponytail on the back of her head makes her look younger, more her age. With the nail apron tied around her waist and hammer in hand, she seems ready to get busy.

"Come over here," I say, making room for her

on my sheet of plywood. "Come see your floor."

"It's really starting to take shape, isn't it?" Leann says breathlessly. She runs her hands over the top of the platform, slowly and reverently, as if it were made out of gold. "The floor in my apartment isn't flat like this one is. Noah's beach ball rolls from one end of the kitchen to the other all by itself."

Never in my life have I seen someone so excited by a floor. Leann does practically everything except dance a little jig on the platform. It's kind of cool to know you're working for someone who will appreciate every little thing you're doing. It makes it all worthwhile.

Jay, Darren, and I feel like zombies at the end of the day, so we head over to the nearest burger joint for dinner. Val meets us there, looking as fresh as a flower after a long day of shopping. I'm not sure why Darren's so wiped out, but my brother and I are bone-deep tired, the kind of tired that comes from a good day's work. It's a relatively unusual sensation for me—the kind of feeling I only get from a long, cold day of skiing or from an afternoon of weeding in Mom's garden. There's a certain dignity in exhausting physical labor.

Man, I must be *really* exhausted. I'm starting to sound like Jayson.

Maybe it was the heat pickling my brain, but today, when I was out there hammering nails, the everyday thoughts that normally occupy my mind started to melt away, and I began thinking about things that never really occurred to me before. I started thinking about what life must've been like a hundred and fifty years ago, when hard labor was a part of everyday life. Everything you needed you had to practically make yourself. If you needed a house, you had to build it. If you needed a dress, you had to sew it. If you needed butter, you had to churn it. Those people back then must've been exhausted all the time, just trying to meet their most basic needs.

"Hey, Space Cadet—how's your burger?"

When I snap back to reality, Val is picking at the crumbs on her plate, staring hungrily at my half-eaten burger. "Is everything okay?"

"Yeah, the burger's great," I say, rubbing my heavy eyelids. "But the milk shake isn't very chocolatey."

Jay's sagging head suddenly perks to attention. "Is that a complaint I hear?"

"I'm not complaining, I'm *commenting*," I answer adamantly. "There was definitely no hint of whining in my voice."

"I suppose . . . ," he agrees, apparently too tired to argue.

Val takes the tall glass from me. "Let me see that shake," she says, quickly draining most of the glass.

Darren is trying to cut into his pork chop by holding it down with the fingers of his right hand and sawing at the piece of meat with a butter knife clutched precariously in his left. I gently take the knife away and cut the meat for him.

"Thanks, Miranda," he says softly, staring at me

in a way that makes my stomach do a somersault.

"The day's practically over, so we might as well call the bet," I say to my brother. "Looks like I won, bro."

"We could go double or nothing," Jay offers, poking at a paper cup of coleslaw with the tines of his fork.

I shake my head furiously. "No way."

"All right." He sighs. "What big favor are you going to ask? Will I have to take you on a huge book-buying spree?"

Darren's still giving me a dreamy-eyed look. "You should make him give you his car."

"Tempting, but I have another idea," I say, easing back in my seat. "I've decided to hold on to my favor for future use."

Jay groans. "Come on, M. Don't leave this hanging over my head. Let's just get it out of the way."

"I'm waiting—winner's prerogative," I answer with authority. "Besides, why blow it on something silly when I might need it for something serious later on?"

Val finishes the shake and snuggles up against Jay. I've noticed that from the moment we stepped in the restaurant, she's been looking at him with big lovey-dovey doe eyes, like the deer we saw up at Big Meadows. I've got an eerie feeling the peal of wedding bells are still ringing in her ears.

"What do you say we take a ride to Sherando

Lake this evening for a moonlight swim?" she says in a husky whisper. "I haven't been there in ages."

Jay exhales loudly. "I'm too tired, Valerie. Some other time."

"We could go see The Waynesboro Players instead—they're doing a production of *Romeo and Juliet*." She toys with the sun-streaked ends of my brother's hair. "You won't have to do a thing but just sit and watch the play."

"I'm really not up for it tonight," Jay insists. The muscles in his jaw tense visibly, like he's ready to snap.

Val rests her head on his shoulder. "I hardly ever see you anymore."

Darren and I stare down at our plates, trying to give the quarreling lovebirds a little psychological distance, but it's hard not to be emotionally involved when Val's pouting like a two-year-old and Jay is as cold as a chunk of marble. It makes me want to stand on the table and shout, *"Stop acting like babies! Have a little respect for us romantically challenged individuals over here!"*

Jay munches sullenly on a fry. "You're not doing anything tomorrow, right? Why don't you come down to the site around my three o'clock break? You could even stay and help out if you wanted to."

"Sorry, can't . . . I just remembered I've got an appointment tomorrow," she says.

"It figures," Jay answers sourly.

The tension between them builds in unbearable silence until Val's eyes light up with an idea. "Why don't you guys come over to my parents' house for lunch Sunday? They've been dying to meet Miranda—and you can come too, Darren, if you want. What do you say?"

The hardening look on my brother's face tells me that this is not exactly his favorite way for them to spend quality time together. The longer it takes him to answer, the more certain I am he's going to say something that will hurt Val's feelings.

"Sounds great to me," I say, stepping in to save her. "What time should we be there?"

So what channel do you want to watch?" Jay asks in a lazy, flat voice, clicking through the channels at about a third of his normal speed. The living room is pitch-dark except for the blistering light of the screen assaulting our eyeballs. We know it's bad to watch TV in the dark, but neither one of us has the energy to lift our arms and turn on a lamp.

"Ugh," I grunt. The exhaustion wracking my body has forced me to resort to a primitive form of communication Jay and I developed when we were younger. At its most basic level, the language consists of one grunt meaning *no* or *I don't care*, and two grunts meaning *yes* or *please pass the chips and salsa*. More sophisticated levels of communication can be achieved through inflection and tone.

"How about the sci-fi movie?" Jay says, sounding like a zombie himself.

"Ugh."

"The Weather Channel?"

"Ugh!"

Jay flinches. "Whoa! You don't have to yell," he says. "How about a rerun of *Gilligan's Island*?"

"Ugh, ugh," I answer with a slight nod.

The phone rings, and Jay and I look at each other in silent debate over who will go pick it up. No one budges. Just as I'm about to grunt about ten reasons why he should do it and not me, Jay climbs out of the chair. "I know, I know," he says, stumbling into the kitchen.

How on earth did the professor manage to make a record player out of coconut shells and bamboo? I wonder in my sleepy stupor. *And where did he get those records, anyway?* The low frequency of Jay's voice blends in with the drone of the TV, drifting, humming, through my head like a swarm of bees. . . .

"It's Mom," Jay says, poking me awake.

"Huh?"

"She's on the phone."

I roll off the couch, my arms and legs like leaden weights. Through slitted eyes I wander into the dim kitchen, bare feet slapping against the floor, the light above the stove gently tracing the outline of the telephone. "Hello?"

"Sorry to wake you, sweetheart . . . " The sound of my mother's tender voice makes me close my eyes and press the receiver against my ear. "I got up because I forgot to lock the back door, and I suddenly had the urge to call you guys."

"That's okay," I answer fuzzily. "How's everything?"

"It's been really quiet around here," she says wistfully. "Your father's had a lot of meetings this week, and Abby's baby-sitting all the time or going out with her friends. She's been treating home like a hotel—to her it's just a place to eat and sleep. I'm afraid your father and I are going to have to tighten the reigns a bit."

I turn on the faucet and pour myself a glass of cold water. "Ahhh . . . to be fourteen again."

"Eighteen's a good age, too," Mom reminds me. "You wouldn't want to go back again, would you?"

"I wouldn't want to have to learn the same lessons over, but things *were* a lot simpler back then," I say.

"Things are a lot simpler now than they will be later on. Just wait until you have children. . . . "

My eyes roll, mostly as a reflex to this familiar speech, but her words resonate at the core of my being. I know she's right—I've seen how it happened to Leann.

"Just wait until you have little Ferdinand and little Penelope running around. . . . "

"Oh, Mom." I groan. "You always pick the worst names."

"That's why I let your father name you kids." Mom laughs. "Jayson told me you're working on a house with him."

I turn one of the kitchen chairs around and sit

144

on it backwards, resting my arms on the back support. "Today was my second day. I didn't think I would like it at all, but it's starting to grow on me. It feels really good to do something worthwhile, you know? Something that will make a difference in someone's life. I had no idea how much work was involved."

"Jayson says you're doing a wonderful job."

"He didn't really say that—"

"Of course he did," Mom insists. "I told him that it didn't surprise me one bit."

I smile to myself, quietly bathing in the shower of my mother's praise. "All I've really done so far is hammer a few nails—anyone can do that."

"Never underestimate yourself, Miranda. There are already plenty of people out there who are willing to do that for you."

We chat about little insignificant things that are of the utmost importance to most mothers whose children have left the nest—what have I been eating, am I getting plenty of rest, do I have fresh underwear. Eventually, Mom cleverly works the conversation around to a topic I knew would make an appearance at some point during the conversation.

"So how long are you and Kirsten staying there?"

I wince. Somewhere along the way I sort of forgot to mention the blowout with Kirsten and that I've gone solo. Well, I haven't really gone solo *yet*, but I'm thinking about it. No use bringing it up and worrying her half to death until I've figured out what's going on. Anything can happen in a few weeks.

Mom continues on. "I really like that you're there with Jayson. You *know* I like you being there."

"I know . . . " I trace invisible patterns on the tabletop with my fingertips. "I think I want to stick around long enough to see the house finished—after that, I'm not sure."

"I guess that means I'll be sleeping easier for the next few weeks," she says with a deep sigh. "I sure miss you kids. You know you can come home anytime you want, right?"

I fold my arms and lay my head down. "I know."

Things are moving fast at the site—so fast, the days are beginning to meld together into one indistinguishable blur. The group I've been working with over the last few days has started the framing—that is, constructing the outside walls with two-by-fours. We actually assemble the walls *on* the subfloor, then raise them into place. There's a second group working on the partitions, or interior walls, which will be moved into position later, before the last exterior wall goes up. We've also left rough openings for doors and windows to be installed later. The wooden skeleton of the house looks so fragile to me—it's amazing that's all there is to it.

Leann made me promise yesterday that we wouldn't raise the first wall without her, so when it looks like we're getting close, I borrow Gary's cell phone and call her at work. Her boss lets her leave early, and she comes right over. The look on her face when she arrives is absolutely electric.

"Thanks for calling me." Leann squeezes my

elbow about four times and has trouble letting go. "Shoot. I meant to bring my camera. I wanted to take pictures."

"We can wait if you want to go get it," I offer.

Leann shakes her head impatiently. "Let's just get on with it. I don't need pictures—this is a moment I'll never forget, anyway."

When Gary gives the signal, we line up and, on the count of three, heave the first wall into place. Jay and a few of the other guys prop up the wall with a piece of timber for temporary support. Applause and shouts of excitement rise up from the crew now that the house is starting to take on a real shape instead of just being a platform on top of cement. Leann presses her fingers to her lips, her soft eyes absorbing every inch of the structure. When no one is looking, I find the heads of all the nails I pounded and run the tip of my finger over each one. *I did this . . . and this . . . and this . . .*

The next step for my group is sheathing, which is nailing plywood sheets to the exterior of the frame. I figure the job will be just like nailing down the subfloor, but it doesn't take long to realize that when you're hammering nails into a floor, you have the advantage of gravity. Nailing something over your head—well, that's a different story.

"I'm finding muscles I never knew existed," huffs Leann, working the sheet next to mine.

"I'm experiencing pain I never knew existed," I groan.

Of course, Jay just happens to be walking by when I say this, and of course he catches every word. "Do I hear someone complaining?" he teases.

"I won the bet—I can complain all I want now," I say, yanking out a crooked nail with my hammer. "So what goes on after the plywood? Some more wood? Cement?"

"No," Jay says, shaking his head. "Just a moisture barrier to keep the rain out, and some shingles. That's about it."

I almost drop my hammer. "You mean you're making this house out of plywood? That's it? You guys really skimp on the materials."

Leann laughs. "They're not skimping—a lot of houses are made with plywood. It's strong stuff."

"Plus, there's going to be insulation and drywall on the inside," Jay adds.

It still doesn't seem like enough to me, but what do I know? I just want to make sure we're making something good, something that will last. Something Leann will treasure for a long time.

"He still keeps talking about you," Leann says, taking a seat on an overturned bucket.

"Who?" I whip my head around, looking for Darren.

"Noah."

"Oh," I say, giggling to myself.

Perspiration glistens on Leann's forehead and collarbone. She takes a drink from her water bottle, then offers me some. "He calls you The Red Lady—I guess he's talking about your hair. Every once in a while, we'll be playing and he'll say, 'Mom—where's The Red Lady?'"

"You should bring him by sometime," I say, grinning. "I'd love to see him again—just leave the peanut butter at home."

A fly lands on Leann's knee, and she shoos it away. "I was thinking about bringing him, but it's too dangerous to have him here with everything going on."

"I could watch him—if you wanted."

"Yeah?" She looks surprised by my offer.

"Yeah," I say. "It'd be fun."

"It's really nice of you to offer," Leann says, her eyes growing moist again. "I'll think about it."

By Saturday I have four blisters, a skinned knee, a sunburn on my nose, the slightest hint of muscle definition in my upper arms, and a splinter in my palm that hasn't quite worked its way out yet. And I love every minute of it.

It'd been so long since I'd dug in and let myself get really dirty that I'd forgotten how much fun it can be. It's so freeing to just roll out of bed in the morning, not caring at all about what you look like or what you're going to wear for the day, and just get outside and create something with your hands. I don't know how it happens, but when you're doing physical labor, all the unimportant stuff gets stripped away and what you're left with is a clearer sense of what really matters. Sometimes it's subtle, and other times, well, it just sort of bangs you over the head in a way that's hard to ignore.

Like yesterday, when I got my splinter.

I was sitting on a scrap piece of plywood, just hanging out, taking a break. My eyes were fixed on the crew because they were putting up the roof trusses and I was curious to see how they were going to do it. Without looking, I reached for my water bottle and, missing it by a mile, accidentally grazed the edge of the board instead. I've never been good with personal injury, and the sight of the brownish-black shard under my skin made me queasy.

At the risk of sounding like a total loser, I have to say that at that moment, I really wished my mom was there with me. She has this great way of taking out splinters so it doesn't hurt a bit. This time, though, I knew I was on my own.

While I was trying to pick the splinter out of my hand with my dirty, stubby fingernails, I kept thinking about the phone conversation I'd had with Mom a few days ago. I thought about how much I missed her and wondered if I was being unfair to her by taking off like this. From the moment I'd decided to leave with Kirsten, all I'd been thinking about was *my* freedom, *my* rights, *my* life. If I'd spent any time at all considering my parents' feelings, it was only to reinforce my assertion that they were being unreasonable and that I understood more about the modern world than they did.

Now I wondered if *I* was the one being unreasonable.

A few weeks ago, what I needed more than anything was to prove to myself that I could leave

Connecticut and spread my wings. Haven't I accomplished that already, even if it's on a smaller scale than I'd originally intended? Before I left home, I'd had dreams of laying under the big western sky, hiking down into the Grand Canyon, taking a train up the California coast. It's wonderful to dream, but it's not real life. In real life, people go to school and get jobs and take care of their responsibilities. People work hard. That's the way it's supposed to be.

So that's why I've decided to go to school.

I haven't told Jay yet, but I've been thinking that as soon as Leann's house is finished, I'll go back home for the rest of the summer and then enroll in Yale in the fall. It doesn't matter that I still don't know what I want to study—I can figure that out when I get there, right? I mean, how many college freshmen really know what they want to do for the rest of their lives?

I'm sure there are some people back home who are going to think I chickened out, but I don't care. I really don't.

I feel good about my decision. I'm young. There's plenty of time for me to see the world. Maybe I'll fly to San Francisco over spring break and visit Chloe. Maybe next summer I'll go to China.

Besides, if I did everything now, what else would I have to look forward to?

We arrive at the Lewises' at noon on the dot. Valerie's parents live in a huge, white-columned plantation-style house in a quiet section of Charlottesville, away from the bustle of the university. From the long, gated driveway the place looks as pretty as a southern postcard with blossoming magnolia trees clustered around the property and a luxurious Virginia lawn rolling out to meet us. Checking my slim brown skirt and white blouse twice for wrinkles, I discreetly hide my surprise. I sort of knew Valerie's family had money, but not *this* much money.

A man, whom I assume to be Mr. Lewis, opens the grand white doors before we even reach the front steps. He's a tall, imposing figure, with deep creases etched into his tanned cheekbones, and dark, magnetic eyes that hold your gaze and never seem to let you go. "Come in! Come in!" he says, his melodious voice laced with charm. "Welcome!"

Jay wipes his palm on the side of his khakis and extends his hand limply to Mr. Lewis, the

corners of his mouth twitching almost imperceptibly. If I didn't know any better, I'd think my
brother was on the verge of a nervous breakdown.

"Good morning—I mean, afternoon . . . sir,"
Jay says, clearing his throat.

"And a beautiful *afternoon,* isn't it?" Mr. Lewis
smiles at me from under the whiskers of his thick
mustache. "I can assume that you must be Jay's sister, Miss Miranda Burke?"

A jolt seizes my brother. "Yeah—sorry . . . I forgot to introduce . . . " his voice trails off in a quiv-
ering puddle of unease. In order to put my brother
out of his misery, I step right up and take over.

"It's a pleasure to meet you," I answer, extend-
ing my hand.

Mr. Lewis takes my hand in his and squeezes
the life out of it. "Preston Lewis," he says, his hypnotic eyes bearing down on me. "The pleasure is
all mine."

We are led into the area Mr. Lewis refers to as
the Grand Foyer, which is truly grand in every
sense of the word. The floor is made of glossy
wood inlaid in a herringbone pattern, and the
milky white walls rise up at least two stories and
then arc overhead, cradling a brass chandelier in
the middle of the cathedral ceiling. A horseshoe-
shaped staircase sweeps dramatically before us up
to a pristine second-floor balcony. I can't even
begin to imagine all the labor and skill it took to
build such a magnificent house.

"Valerie will be joining us shortly," Mr. Lewis says, showing us to the formal parlor straight ahead, the heels of his polished shoes clicking against the floor. Large crystal vases filled with fresh flowers decorate antique tabletops, and sheer white drapes diffuse the sunlight coming through the French doors leading to the terrace. Through the gauzy fabric I see blurred, Impressionistic patches of green grass and blue sky.

Jay takes a seat in a creaky, claw-footed chair and quietly sweats.

"You have a lovely home," I say, crossing my legs demurely. As much as I love the simpler things in life, I think I could get used to this.

"Thank you very much," Mr. Lewis answers graciously. "It was built by my ancestor, Colonel Walter Lewis, of Manchester, England, in seventeen forty-two." He sidles up to the old marble fireplace and points to a stone in the center, engraved with words I can hardly make out. "This is the text of the original land grant Colonel Lewis received from—"

"Dad, you're not boring them with that, are you?" Valerie interrupts as she bounds into the room. She looks beautiful in a knee-length lilac skirt and matching sleeveless top, and her hair is loosely braided down her back. Jay stands up, and she kisses him, a little longer and a little more intensely than I would feel comfortable doing with a parent in the room. Mr. Lewis looks away and clears his throat, dusting the surface of his land grant stone with the cuff of his brass-buttoned blazer.

"Thanks for coming," Valerie says to me when she finally pulls herself off my brother's lips. She takes me by the hand. "Dinner will be ready soon. I'll give Miranda the tour while you two chat."

Mr. Lewis's face lights up. "I don't believe Jay has heard about Colonel Lewis's exploits as a tobacco farmer . . . "

I can almost feel the dread settling in the center of Jay's chest. The helpless look on his face makes me stop in my tracks.

"Come *on*," Valerie coaxes, pulling my arms. "I want to show you something."

So? What do you think?"

"I . . . uh . . . I . . ." My tongue feels too thick to speak. I brace myself against the brocade walls of Valerie's room and try again. "I thought you were going to be cool about this."

"I *am* cool." Valerie's smile dissolves as she pulls the hanger away from her body. "So you're saying you don't like it?"

"No . . . no . . . it's gorgeous." I cover my face with my hands and groan.

I am such *dead meat.*

Valerie hangs the gown on the back of her door, the yards of silk and intricate embroidery tumbling down around her feet. "It's not like I planned for this to happen. I went to this vintage clothing store, and there it was. I was just trying it on for fun, and it fit perfectly. I mean perfectly. The sales guy said he'd never seen such a perfect fit. He says it was worn by an Austrian princess—I don't know how true that is, but it sounds good. Some people have a hang-up about wearing someone else's wedding gown, but it doesn't bother me a bit."

"Doesn't it bother you that you have the dress but you don't even have the *groom* yet?"

"It's a one-of-a-kind dress. How could I pass it up?" Valerie sees the traumatic look on my face, and her eyes soften. "I can always dye it black, cut off the train, and wear it as a party dress. Hey, don't worry, my parents have money to burn—this is not a problem."

My legs give way, and I sink down to the plush white carpeting. "You told them?"

Valerie looks away sheepishly. "Not in so many words. I couldn't help it—they saw me bring the dress home."

"This is not good. . . . " A painful spasm sears my stomach, and I double over. I can only imagine what my brother and Mr. Lewis are *really* talking about at this very moment—mortgages, life insurance, the cost of private school tuition. "Jay is going to murder me when he finds out I told you."

Val disappears into her walk-in closet and comes out with a triple-tiered wedding veil complete with silk roses. "Don't you think you're overreacting a little?" she says, draping the veil over her head. "I've known all along that Jay and I would be married someday, even before you said anything. We could be married a year from now or ten years from now, it doesn't matter. So what if I bought my dress a little on the early side? It's one less thing I'll have to think about."

Even though her words sound levelheaded and rational, there's something in Val's eyes that tells me she just isn't getting it. "The reason why I even mentioned that Jay was saving up for a ring was because you were feeling down and I wanted you to feel secure about your relationship. I never thought you'd . . . start making plans."

"It takes a year or two to plan a big wedding, Miranda," she says with authority. "It's never too early to start thinking about what you want."

What about what my brother wants?

Val pulls an accordion file full of bridal magazine clippings out of her desk and dumps them in the middle of her bed. "Take a look at *these*," she says, pulling out samples of bridesmaid dresses. "Do you like?"

"They're beautiful . . . " I sigh, afraid to look. My reluctant eye catches a glimpse of an elegant sapphire formal with a square neckline and spaghetti straps. It's so gorgeous, it actually gives me a chill. "I really like this one."

"Me, too," Val says dreamily. "I bet it'd look great on you."

"It'd probably be all right," I answer, sifting through the clippings, thinking of all the ways I'm going to have to ask my brother for forgiveness when he figures out what I've done. I could promise to clean his dorm room every day for a year or take care of his laundry or something equally repulsive if that's what it takes. Then again, who knows—maybe he'll be so glad I'm going back to school, it won't matter to him that I was indiscreet. Maybe he'll be glad I broke the ice for him because he was too scared to broach the subject on his own.

Oooooo . . . that's a good argument. I'll have to remember that one when he's screaming his guts out at me.

"I have to say, I was hoping for a little more support from you, since you're going to be my sister-in-law and all, but I'm not mad or anything," Val says, giving me a close hug. "I'd still love for you to be my bridesmaid."

Now it's my turn to sweat.

In the short time Val and I have been gone discussing premature wedding plans, my poor brother manages to turn three shades of white and starts to work on a translucent shade of blue. The second I see him, my stomach caves in, figuring Mr. Lewis must've taken the opportunity to grill Jay during their time alone, but judging from the small smile of relief on his face when we return, I suspect that maybe it was just all that talk of tobacco farming that made him nauseous.

"How are you holding up?" I whisper to him as we make our way down the long hall to the formal dining room. "Is everything all right?"

Jay loosens his necktie a smidgen. "If I pass out at the table, just prop me up in my seat. Maybe no one will notice."

In the dining room, Mrs. Lewis is already seated at the head of the formal table in a state of relaxed casualness more suited to someone who is about to finish a meal rather than start one. She has the same dark, flowing hair as her daughter, though clearly the color has been chemically enhanced. Her skin is smooth like porcelain and finely preserved for a woman of her age. She's beautiful in a well-kept sort of way.

"It's so nice to see you again, Jayson," Mrs. Lewis says in a throaty voice, between sips from a water goblet. "Welcome, Miranda."

"Hi, Mrs. Lewis," Jay breathes soberly.

I venture a polite smile. Valerie's mother returns an equally polite smile and motions for us to take our seats—me on one side of the dining table, Val and Jay on the other, Mr. Lewis at the other end. There is an uneasy quiet in the room. Jay clears his throat a half dozen times, the sound echoing off the massive walls. I inspect my own personal collection of polished silverware lined up on either side of my plate like a surgeon's tray, leaving me to wonder if we're supposed to dissect the food instead of eat it.

"We're having crown roast," Mrs. Lewis announces. A moment later, a small, butterball of a woman in a chef's uniform comes out of the kitchen carrying dinner on an artfully arranged silver platter. No sooner is the lovely roast placed on the table than it is quickly dismantled and divided among the five of us. The Lewises dig in with a lack of ceremony that seems misplaced in such an elegant dining room.

"Jay and Miranda are almost done with their

first house," Valerie announces, glancing at both parents. "I haven't seen it yet, but I hear it's nice."

Mr. Lewis spears a piece of meat and sets his eyes on me. "You're involved in that volunteer group, too, Miranda?"

"Yes," I answer, trapped by his gaze. "It's a lot of fun."

"I've never cared much for all that bleeding heart business, myself," he says. "Common sense tells you that if someone wants a house, they should build the damn thing themselves and not rely on someone else to do it for them. That's how Colonel Lewis did it. He wouldn't ask for a handout. I dare you to find any place in Colonel Lewis's journal that says, 'I need a house. I really wish someone would build it for me.'"

My cheeks start to burn. Jay carefully places his fork on the edge of his plate and raises his head, looking in Mr. Lewis's direction, but still not squarely in the eye. "The families we work with take part in the building and then they buy them from the organization," he says. "We like to think of it as a hand *up*, not a hand *out*."

Mrs. Lewis presses her glossed lips tightly together and casts a syrupy look at Jay as if to say, *"Isn't he just the most precious thing you've ever seen? He really believes in all that compassionate nonsense."* My sibling radar goes off, detecting a tremor of gigantic proportions rumbling beneath the surface of my brother's skin, like hot magma

164

pushing up through a volcano. If there's one thing that drives my brother ballistic, it's not being taken seriously.

Valerie puts her hand on Jay's knee and diffuses the fire a little. "Gee, I'm sorry I brought it up," she says heavily, with a sideways glance to her father. "I think what Jay is doing is very noble and worthwhile."

Mr. Lewis gives Jay a condescending smirk, the kind of smirk some older people like to give when they think they're being funny or helpful, when in fact they're just about to tear you down. "You should've told me you were going to throw away the whole summer working for free, Jay. I could've set you up at one of my newspapers. To use your words, we could always use a hand *up*."

Who does this guy think he is, trashing my brother like that?

"That's enough, Daddy," Valerie hisses through gritted teeth.

"I should've made you go to William and Mary instead of that school up north, Valerie," Mr. Lewis says. "You're picking up some bad Yankee habits."

The silence that falls over the table is a welcomed relief, especially for Jay, whose composure is disintegrating rapidly. Mrs. Lewis tells us about dessert, some flaky something-or-other that took the chef four hours to make. Then, out of the blue, she says something that almost makes me fall out of my chair. "I love strawberries, don't you, Jay?

165

Especially with a nice yellow sponge cake and fresh whipped cream—I think it would make a perfect wedding cake for a summer ceremony, don't you?"

"I don't know," Jay murmurs, his eyes clouding with confusion. "I suppose so . . . "

A blistering fever scorches my skin. *Is the room spinning? I swear it's moving.* . . . Bracing myself against the edge of the table, I watch in horror as Mr. Lewis opens his mouth to speak, wondering what's going to come out next. "What exactly are your prospects, Jay?" Mr. Lewis asks, placing his napkin beside his plate. "It's never too soon to start planning for the future—especially when it involves my daughter."

"Daddy—" Valerie warns through gritted teeth.

"Valerie's a wonderful young woman—I'm sure you know that already. I'm sure you know, too, that the standard of living she's accustomed to is a bit more extravagant than most people's. She needs a husband who can provide a good life for her—"

"Stop talking like I'm not in the room . . . ," Val cuts in, her eyes growing dark.

Mr. Lewis continues on, as if he doesn't hear her. "I'm not saying you're not capable of taking care of my daughter. All I'm saying is that since you and Valerie are making plans, you ought to be working toward your future instead of volunteering your life away."

166

The fire on the surface of my skin seeps down into my muscles and bones, stinging like acid. *This is all because of my big mouth*, I tell myself. *I am the absolute worst sister on the planet.*

"Excuse me," Jay says, his complexion taking an odd turn from pale to red. "I'm not exactly sure what you mean. What *plans* are you talking about?"

Mrs. Lewis smiles broadly. "The wedding plans, of course," she says. "For your marriage."

Valerie bites her bottom lip and looks at Jay expectantly.

"It's important to start thinking like a family man," Mr. Lewis says. "Maintaining a residence like this may look easy, but I'll assure you it's not. I'll not have my daughter settle for anything less than what her mother and I were able to provide for her. Do you understand?"

I grit my teeth and hang on to the edge of the table for dear life, waiting for the volcano to explode, but Jay simply closes his eyes. Valerie and I exchanged worried glances, but a moment later Jay seems to regain his composure.

"It was a lovely dinner, Mrs. Lewis," Jay says, taking a sip of water. "But I'm afraid I won't be able to stay for dessert."

We all watch in stunned silence as my brother stands up and walks right out the door.

This is definitely not one of my better days. I've been sitting in Jay's car for what seems like an hour, wiping my damp palms on the upholstery while he has it out with Valerie. I can see them in the side mirror, sitting on an iron bench under one of the magnolia trees, the orange light of late afternoon shining on their faces. Valerie's been talking a lot and crying, while Jay keeps running his hands through his hair and shaking his head. I wonder if my name's come up in the conversation. It's hard to tell—I can't read lips from here.

Finally, Jay stands up and starts walking toward the car, but Val grabs his arm and holds him back. He says something that makes her let go, then he continues on toward the car with his jaw hard and tense. There's a cold feeling in the pit of my stomach that tells me something terrible has just happened.

My brother doesn't say a thing as we pull away from the house, his hands locked on the steering wheel, his arms as rigid as stone. His face is vacant and unresponsive. *He hates me . . . he hates me . . .* the words run endlessly through my head. He's never going to talk to me again. And I can't say I blame him.

As we near the end of the long driveway, the car comes to a gentle halt and stands there, idling. I look over at Jay and see his lips tremble and his jaw go slack, then the tears start to flow. He grips the steering harder until his knuckles whiten, managing to hold himself together for a moment longer before completely disintegrating right in front of me.

Without saying a word, I reach my arms out to Jay and let him rest his head on my shoulder.

"Sorry I took off," he finally says in a shaky voice. "I felt like the room was closing in on me back there."

I stare straight ahead through the windshield, watching cars on the main road rushing past. "Her parents are pretty demanding people."

"If it was just them, I could handle it . . . ," he trails off. "Do you know she even bought a wedding dress?"

My heart sinks. "She showed me when we were upstairs."

"We're only halfway through school, M. I'm not ready to get married yet—I don't even know if she's the person I want to marry."

I swallow hard. "I thought you were sure about Valerie. You told me at Thanksgiving that you could see yourself spending the rest of your life with her."

Jay sits up and wipes his red eyes with the back of his hand. "I don't know. She seems different here. At school she seems easygoing and down-to-earth. Here, she's like a princess living in a castle. Mr. Lewis is right, you know—how could I ever make her happy?" He sighs a deep, gut-wrenching sigh and stares out the window. "The Valerie I know is secure and confident, not obsessive and needy. And that wedding dress—the Val I know would never do something like that. What made her change?"

He doesn't know it was me. . . . He doesn't know it's my fault. A lump swells in my throat at the realization that Val could've ratted on me to save herself, but she didn't. She's probably hoping I'll tell him myself—I definitely owe it to her. And I owe it to my brother, too.

You know, Jay, remember that day Val took me to the park? Well, a funny thing happened . . . yeah, Val thought you didn't love her anymore, so I told her you were going to propose to her, because I sort of thought you were going to do it even though I didn't have any real proof and I thought it would make Val feel better. Oooops! I know it probably doesn't seem very funny to you right now, but give it a few days. . . .

There's no easy way to admit when you've been a thoughtless jerk.

"You know, Jay . . . ," I start, when my windpipe tightens suddenly, squeezing off my breath. It's obvious my body is trying to tell me something. This is not the right time to confess—I need to give him a little time to recover from the afternoon. Tonight. I'll tell him tonight.

"What?" he asks.

My throat relaxes, and I'm able to speak again. "Sometimes people get weird when they go home to their parents'—they start acting like kids again. I know if Mr. and Mrs. Lewis were *my* parents, I'd be a nutball."

That's not exactly what I meant to say, but I think Jay gets the gist of it.

"Just cut her a little slack, that's all," I add.

"Don't worry," Jay says, stepping on the gas. "I'm cutting her slack, all right. I'm giving her all the slack she needs."

Looks like Darren has some company," Jay says, pulling up to the curb because his parking space is taken by a dumpy blue Ford Escort. "Who in the world does he know from New Jersey?"

"Oh, God, tell me this isn't happening," I mumble to myself, sinking lower and lower in my seat until I'm practically kneeling on the floor mat. *I could be wrong. . . . It might be just a crazy cosmic coincidence that someone with the same blue car with New Jersey plates is parked in our driveway. . . .*

Still, I'm not taking any chances.

"What's wrong with you?" Jay looks down at me, a puddle of nerves on the floor.

I put my hands on my stomach. "Dinner made me feel kind of weird. Could we go to the drugstore and get something?"

"I've got some stuff in the medicine cabinet," he says, cutting the engine.

"Is it still good?" I raise my head a little and peer over the dashboard. "I won't take it if it's expired."

Jay opens the door. "It has a shelf life of a hundred years. It'll last longer than you."

"Milk! What about milk? I think we're almost out . . . ," I say in a last-ditch effort to buy time. "I know how much it ticks you off to wake up in the morning and find out there's no milk in the house. Let's go to Food Lion and get some. While we're at it, we could get our shopping done for the week. . . . "

"We can go later." My brother scrunches his forehead so hard, his eyebrows almost touch, indicating to me that I'm pushing my luck. "Quit the neurotic routine—okay, M? It's been a tough day."

This might just be a dream, I tell myself to suppress the tingling panic that's rising in the base of my spine. Maybe I'm having an anxiety dream like the ones I had before graduation where I walk up to the podium in my cap and gown to receive my diploma, only to find out there's been a mistake in the records and I have to do high school all over again.

Come on, wake up . . . I close my eyes, hoping desperately that when I open them again, I'll be stretched out on the couch, buried under a pile of blankets, and this whole day will have been nothing more than a really bad dream. But when I open my eyes, the car is still there and Jay is by the front door waving his arms, looking at me like I'm psycho.

So much for wishful thinking. I crawl out of the

Saturn like a circus clown coming out of a miniature police car and make my way up the path, taking a slight detour around the perimeter of the suspicious blue vehicle. Through the sunlit glare of the back window I look for clues, but aside from a pair of old blue jeans and a mountain of fast-food wrappers, I can't see all that much. If I really want to know who this car belongs to, I'm going to have to do some digging.

Check the glove box. . . . The registration should be in there.

Jay sighs. "Are you coming or not?"

Before I have a chance to answer, the driver's side of the door swings open, and a pair of bare feet lazily find their way to the open air, followed by outstretched legs and a torso rolling sleepily in the reclined seat. "Oh, there you are," Kirsten yawns, barely lifting her head. "I was wondering when you were coming back."

What are *you* doing here?" I demand, while my jaw goes slack and my body grows numb. It feels as though the ground under my feet has opened up and swallowed me, and in a way I wish it would. Or better yet, I wish it would swallow *her* instead. "How'd you find me?"

"Jeez, Miranda, you sound like you're in a witness relocation program," Kirsten says, combing her fingers through her black, shoulder-length hair. She spots Jay by the door to the apartment and gives him a cutesy wave and a pouty smile. "I called your mom, and she told me you were here. She seemed pretty confused at first that we weren't together. Then I figured out that you hadn't told her yet—naughty, naughty," she says, shaking a finger at me. "Don't worry, though, I covered for you. I made up some melodramatic story like I went for a drive in the mountains and had a sudden case of amnesia, and her phone number was the only one in my pocket."

I don't care for the way Kirsten is making my

mom sound like a sucker, and I care even less for the flirtatious glances she keeps sending in Jay's direction. Speaking of my brother, in all of three seconds he's instantly switched gears from Mr. Depressed to Super-Happy Personality Man. The next thing I know, he's standing by the car door, nudging me aside, with this great big, goofy grin on his face.

"Kirsten, how've you been?" Jay opens his arms wide, and she, of course, jumps right into them, wrapping herself around him like a Slinky. "It's been so long."

"I know," she answers in a husky voice. "I thought I was going to see you when your parents dropped Miranda off, but they told me you were here, saving the world."

Jay blushes. "I'm just building some houses, that's all."

Does she have to talk to him three inches from his face? She's clutching him like she's drowning in the ocean and he's the only life preserver around. How desperate. I mean, really, get a hold of yourself, woman. Children live next door. And to think Jay was only her chemistry partner in high school—I'd hate to see how she acts around old boyfriends.

I clear my throat—loudly. "How's your mother doing?"

"Ugh. You would have to bring the party down." Kirsten releases Jay from her death grip and takes a seat on the hood of the car. "Things were all right for a couple of days after you left; then when the tourists started streaming in, she got all stressed out."

"Running a bed-and-breakfast isn't the easiest job in the world," I remind her.

"That's what *she* kept saying! Boy, you guys think alike." Kirsten regards me with an amused smirk. "Anyway, we were getting on each other's nerves like crazy—especially since we were living in that small room together. It wasn't working at all, so I decided I'd had enough of a good time."

One of the things that amazed me about Kirsten when I was staying with her in New York was her inability to get attached to places, things, or even people. Just before we left for our trip that never ended up happening, I watched her say good-bye to dozens of friends without her so much as shedding a tear or giving them a regretful smile. Even as we were leaving New York, her home for the past two years, she preferred to sleep on the bus instead of indulging in sentimentality. I really admired that quality—her ability to easily sever ties that were holding her back. That is, until I became one of the people she cut loose.

"So where are you living now?" Jay asks.

Kirsten shrugs. "Out of my car, I guess. I haven't given it much thought."

Yeah, right. "There are some cheap campgrounds near the park," I suggest.

Jay scowls at me. "Forget the campgrounds. She can stay here with us."

"There isn't a lot of room," I protest, talking only to Jay. "I don't think Kirsten would want to sleep on the floor."

"Oh, I don't mind—"

"And we have to think of Darren," I continue on. "It's his apartment, too."

"Are you talking about the guy with the cast?" Kirsten asks, her blue eyes wide and innocent looking. "I talked to him already, and he seems really nice. Of course, I wouldn't want to cause a problem. . . . "

Jay shakes his head. "There's no problem at all. We'd love to have you stay with us." He says this with such finality that it's clear there's no room for further protest.

"That'd be cool," she says, laying it on thick with a girlie smile. "It won't be for very long. As soon as Miranda's ready to go, we'll be on our way."

One afternoon, when the guy is at the beach, I'm walking down the hallway and there's the same horrible odor coming from his room again. This time, I vow to find out the source of the hideous smell," Kirsten says, pausing for drama. "So I key into his room."

"You didn't!" Jay leans forward on the kitchen table, drinking in her every word.

Darren twitches in his seat. "What happened?"

Oh, yes, Kirsten, I think dryly. *Please tell us everything.*

Kirsten takes a leisurely sip of her black coffee, enjoying her moment—or should I say *two hours*—in the spotlight. "I unlocked the door, turned the knob slowly, and when I flicked on the light switch, guess what I saw."

"A week-old pizza," Jay says.

"A dead body?" Darren chirps.

A button that says, ASK ME IF I CARE.

"A monkey." Kirsten beams. "Can you believe it? There was a monkey in the room!"

"A monkey?" Darren and Jay say in unison. Boy, does she have them trained like house pets. Every few minutes she rewards them with a coy little laugh or an alluring glance, just enough to keep them begging for more.

If only they knew her like I did. Then they wouldn't be wagging their tongues so much.

"But that's not the funny part." Kirsten tries to contain her laughter. "The guy had left the monkey's cage door open, and the animal was hanging from the curtain rod by his tail! And he left a nice yellow streak down one side of my mother's antique linen curtains that she didn't appreciate!"

Jay and Darren absolutely roar.

"That's gross," I say soberly. "Not to mention unsanitary."

Darren staggers across the kitchen floor toward the coffeemaker, holding his cast against his stomach. "A monkey!"

"Are you sure you can handle that by yourself?" I ask, watching him shake with laughter as he pours himself another cup of coffee. The lip of the coffeepot is banging unsteadily against the rim of the mug, a typical Darren move.

"I'm fine," he answers dismissively. His eyes are glued to you-know-who.

Kirsten gives her hair a predictable toss. "It turns out that the guy didn't bring the monkey along as a pet—he's the head of some exotic animal smuggling ring that was wanted by the FBI."

Oh, please . . .

"That's incredible," my brother says, buying the ridiculous story.

You're a smart person, Jay. I'd expect more from you.

Darren skips back to the table with his mug of hot coffee. "How did you find—ow, ow, ow!" His eyes bulge, and his face turns bright red.

"Oh, God, Darren! What did you do?" I ask, rushing to his side in time to see a scalding brown river of coffee trickle down inside his cast. "How'd you do that?"

Biting down hard on his lower lip, Darren shakes his head, unable to answer.

"Get some ice!" I shout at Jay, who's already three-quarters of the way to the freezer as I mop up some of the excess liquid with a dishcloth.

"Let me see," Kirsten says, shoving me aside and taking Darren over to the kitchen sink.

"He's not supposed to get his cast wet," I tell Kirsten, but she doesn't listen to me.

"It doesn't matter—the coffee's made it wet already." She aims the spout into the thumbhole of Darren's cast, squirting water everywhere. "How's that?"

"Better," Darren sighs, a slight smile returning to his face. "Thanks so much, Kirsten."

Yeah . . . thanks a whole bunch. I toss the dishcloth on the kitchen table and walk out.

When Kirsten settles down for the night on the living room floor, I'm buried under the covers with my nose pressed against the couch's dusty upholstery, exaggerating my breathing like I'm already asleep so she'll leave me alone.

"Here's the only extra blanket I have," Jay whispers to her while they move the coffee table aside. "Tomorrow we'll get Miranda to give up one of hers."

Fat chance. I clench a fistful of the top comforter in case he decides to steal one.

"This will be fine—really," she says, talking just as loudly as she did in the kitchen when she impressed us all with her sparkling wit.

Do you mind? Some people are trying to sleep here.

"Okay . . . Are you sure you don't want to use my bed instead? I don't mind sleeping on the floor at all," Jay whispers.

There's a loud *thump*, which I assume is

Kirsten flopping unceremoniously on the floor. Exhaling through my nose, I keep pretending to be asleep, even though no normal human being could've stayed asleep through so many rude interruptions.

"Thanks, Jay, but this is fine," she says. "It's kind of like a slumber party."

How cute.

After they say good night to each other and the light goes off, I open my eyes to the darkness and roll over slowly so Kirsten won't hear me. Even though she's on the other side of the room, lying silently in the dark, Kirsten's presence is still oppressive and overwhelming, pushing at me without even trying, rubbing my nerves raw. She just takes up so much *space.*

"I guess I should've called first, huh?"

Is she talking to me? My instinct is not to answer, to continue pretending that I'm asleep, but Kirsten's confident tone of voice tells me she's not fooled one bit by my acting.

"It would've been nice," I say quietly.

"I thought about it once or twice but figured it would be a lot more fun to see the look on your face when I showed up." There's a dull punching sound coming from Kirsten's side of the room, like she's trying to fluff her pillow. "And it *was* pretty interesting, to say the least. I think you would've been happier to see a rabid dog sitting on your doorstep."

Rabid animals do have their good points—you on the other hand . . .

"You need an outlet for your anger," she adds. "Maybe you should take up kick boxing."

"What anger?" I bark.

Kirsten is silent just long enough to let the echo of my own voice drive her point home. "The last time I saw you, you said you weren't mad at me anymore."

"I lied, all right? I think I'm entitled to feel betrayed. . . . " I throw off the covers, feeling like the entire surface of my body is sizzling under a broiler.

"Be mad if you want, but I'm here now, ready to pick the trip up where we left off," she says. "I'm here to make things right again."

"You're here because you had a fight with your mother and you didn't know where else to go." Something snaps inside me, and the emotional floodgates are bursting open. I can't hold back now, even if I tried. "I was your backup plan. You figured I was too lame to take the trip by myself, so if things didn't work out in Cape May, I wouldn't be too far away, just waiting for you to come back."

Without warning, Kirsten turns on one of the table lamps, leaving me blinded by the sudden burst of unexpected light. "I'm flattered you think I'm so conniving, but to be honest, my motivations are hardly that sophisticated," she says coolly. "I needed a place to go and I thought of you."

If you needed a place to go, why did you drive hours to get here when you could've gone back to your roommate, Vance, in New York City? The question burns a hole in my stomach, but I keep the argument to myself.

"And I didn't think you were lame at all," Kirsten adds. "In fact, I was pretty sure I'd get here too late to hook up with you—I thought you'd be in California by now."

I'm so flattered that she thinks I'm adventurous that my defenses start to break down. "Well, there's been a change of plans."

"Oh?"

"I'm going to stick around to finish the house I'm working on, then I'm going back to Connecticut." I stop for a second, slightly taken aback by the firm tone of my own voice. When did I ever get so confident and self-assured? Do I mean what I'm saying or am I just trying to impress Kirsten?

"I'm going to Yale in the fall," I finish.

While Kirsten takes a moment to absorb the news, I stare down at her from my perch on the couch, feeling a bit like a queen admonishing one of her lowly subjects. For the first time, *I'm* the one in control of the situation. *I'm* the one dictating the rules. *I* have the power. And, I have to say, it feels pretty darn good.

Kirsten frowns at the floor, hugging her knees and rocking slowly from side to side. Then, she stares right back at me with a look of complete ambivalence. "Hey, you've gotta do what you've gotta do," she says, clicking off the light. Not even sixty seconds go by before she's settled into a steady pattern of deep, restful snoring, while I'm staring at the black ceiling.

That's it? I wonder, burying myself deeper under the covers. *She's not even going to try to talk me out of it?*

When Jay, Darren, and I leave for the site the next morning, Kirsten insists on coming along. I'm dead set against it, figuring she'll just goof around and not get any work done, but I'm overruled by The Hormone Twins, who of course think it's a brilliant idea to watch her run around all day in cutoffs and a tank top.

I don't really care if Darren wags his tongue at her or not—I really don't—but Jay worries me. From the moment Kirsten slinked out of her beat-up car, all thoughts of Valerie seemed to have permanently evaporated from his consciousness. Maybe *some* guys are capable of being so easily sidetracked, but not my brother. It's not natural for him. I don't care how bad things went at the Lewises' yesterday, Jay just can't turn his feelings off for Val like a light switch, even if Kirsten is beautiful and exciting and maybe even a little bit dangerous. I'm hoping she's nothing more than a distraction for him while he recovers, but my gut tells me that if he doesn't watch it—well, I don't even want to think about *that*.

Now that the walls and the roof are up, things are moving very swiftly, and we're rewarded almost hourly with visible progress. Van loads of enthusiastic people from local church groups come by to help us tack up the wooden shingling, while the regular crew finishes installing windows and the outside window trim. The licensed electrician starts wiring the house, but we run into a little snag when the plumber doesn't show up. Luckily, Gary knows someone who is more than happy to donate his time to help us out, and we lose almost no time at all.

I'm on my second row of shingles when Leann appears beside me, holding Noah's hand. Her hair is tied back in a hasty bun, and her eyes are sunk deeply in their sockets. "Can I talk to you for a second?" she says.

There's something in her voice that gives me a slight chill, even though it's nearly ninety degrees out here. "Sure," I answer. Stopping with a nail still sticking out of the shingle, I take Noah's other hand as we walk over to the soda cooler. "What's wrong?"

"Someone tried to get into my apartment last night," Leann says, sitting down on the grass and pulling her son onto her lap.

I swallow hard. "Oh, no—are you all right?"

Leann nods slowly. "Just a little shaken up is all. I needed to tell somebody—but I didn't want everybody to know." A tear forms in the corner of her eye but is quickly wiped away. "It's no big deal, really. Some drunk guy was looking for his girl-friend and had the wrong apartment. He screamed for two hours and tried to break down the door. I called 911, but it took them forever to come."

It's so unfair . . . Leann never catches a break. I put my arm around her in an awkward hug. Noah reaches up and grabs onto the end of my ponytail. "You must've been scared out of your mind," I say.

"Oh, I wasn't worried about him getting in," Leann says, gaining her composure. "I had practi-cally every stick of furniture in the apartment pushed up against the door. What made me mad was that he woke up my baby." She brushes Noah's wispy bangs off his damp forehead while he tries to wriggle out of her arms. "The whole time Noah and I were locked up in the bedroom, praying the man would go away, I kept thinking, *the house is almost finished. Noah has somewhere better to go.* I'll tell you, if I didn't have the new house to get me through, I probably would've lost my mind a long time ago."

"You're not going back there, are you? You can't . . . "

"A friend of mine from work offered to take us in until the house is ready." Leann sighs. "I really hate imposing on people, but there's no way I'm spending another night in that dump."

I sigh, too. "Glad to hear it."

She pours Noah a cup of lemonade and one for herself. "Remember a few days ago when you said you wouldn't mind looking after Noah again? I was kind of wondering if I could take you up on that offer this afternoon."

"Sure."

"I've moved out most of our things already, but there's a little more to do and it would go a lot faster if I didn't have to worry about what he's getting into."

"Of course," I say. "I understand. Take as long as you need."

The edges of Leann's lips are drawn into a tired smile. "For the thousandth time, thank you. I have to say, Miranda, I'm really looking forward to the day when I don't have to keep asking people for favors. And that day's coming soon. I can feel it."

Dis!" Noah shrieks with joy as he attempts to stuff a rusted nail into his mouth.

"Oh, no, you don't . . . " Adrenaline pulses through my veins as I thwart the little guy's plans. With wood beams, tools, and tiny pieces of hardware scattered all over the place, the work site is a minefield for kids. "Let's get out of here," I say, scooping Noah up and bringing him to the tree line on the edge of the lot, safely out of the way.

Noah balances himself between two gnarled roots and points to a fuzzy yellow-and-black-striped caterpillar inching its way up the trunk of the tree. "Dat?"

"Caterpillar," I say. "It's a caterpillar."

"Ca-pil-er," he repeats.

While Noah is transfixed by the wonders of nature, I spy on Kirsten to see what she's up to. It's been a while since I've seen her, which I suspect is because she's napping in the grass somewhere, working on her perpetual tan. But she surprises me. Instead of slacking off like I expected, she's shingling the roof with Marcy and Jay. It's not one of the easiest jobs, especially in this heat, and she's actually working, which is the biggest surprise of all. It's hard to tell from this far away, but Kirsten seems really comfortable up there on the roof, like she's been shingling her whole life. She yells something down to a few of the new volunteers on the ground—I can't make out what she's saying, but everyone laughs. Her first day, and already she's charmed the pants off the whole crew. I've never met anyone who is so adaptable to every situation, who can feel like they belong no matter where they are or who they're with. It must be great to be so comfortable in your own skin.

The owner of the variety store down the street is nice enough to come by and donate a case of ice-cream bars for the whole crew, which everyone wolfs down in a hurry before they melt. I give Noah mine even though he already has one of his own, as if somehow an extra ice cream could make up for what he had to go through last night. Noah happily laps at one Creamsicle dripping down his pudgy arm, and the other he uses to paint tree bark. I watch the little artist decorate trees with his magical orange paintbrush until his mother returns from moving, exhausted but relieved.

Instead of being zonked at the end of the day like he usually is, Jay is a wide-eyed bundle of energy and just can't stop talking. If he's not talking about construction, he's spouting off historical facts about the area or practicing his rather lame repertoire of jokes on Kirsten. She laughs at every single one, no matter how stupid, and pretends she doesn't know the punch line even when it's painfully obvious. I thought Jay hated it when girls acted ditzy, but I guess even the most forward-thinking guys are suckers for women who make them believe they're funnier than they really are.

"Let's go to Sherando Lake," Jay says on the drive home. "I'm in the mood for a swim."

"Sounds great," Kirsten calls from the back seat.

I shoot a heavy look in my brother's direction, but he doesn't pick up on it. Has Kirsten clogged Jay's brain so much that he's forgotten how Val had practically begged him to go to Sherando last week but he'd refused? And now he wants to go with another girl? How insane is that? Is he even going to attempt to patch things up with Val, or is he just going to give up without really trying?

Actually, I think it's my fault. I still haven't told him everything. I've wanted to, but we haven't had five minutes alone since Kirsten got here. Plus, I'm chicken. Things have been really good between us, and I'd hate to screw it up.

We get to the lake around sunset, and Jay's the first one in. He runs in up to about waist high, then dives under, resurfacing several yards out.

"Oh, man! The water's perfect!" Jay shakes his wet head and treads water, his movements making smooth ripples on the glassy lake.

Kirsten, who claims she doesn't own a swimsuit, wades into the water in her cutoffs and tank top. Jay splashes water at her, but Kirsten dives in and does an underwater handstand, kicking her legs defiantly.

Even though I changed into my electric-blue racer-back swimsuit, for some reason the water doesn't tempt me. Perhaps I'd be more apt to go in if Jay and Kirsten weren't having so much fun flirting. If I go in the water, it's almost like saying I'm okay with everything—which I'm not. Instead, I'd rather sit here on this rock in silent protest— saying nothing while stating my position loud and clear.

"Stop it!" Kirsten squeals, shielding herself from Jay's playful splashes. He goes underwater again. "Let go of my ankles!" she screams.

This is so embarrassing, I think to myself. A man fishing in an aluminum boat and a family barbecuing hot dogs nearby all stop and glance in our direction. *Don't look at me—I've never seen these people before in my life. . . .*

"Hey, M, aren't you coming in?" Jay asks, looking right at me.

Thanks for blowing my cover.

"Not right now," I answer, hugging my knees to my chest. A mosquito lands on my forearm, and I watch with curious detachment as it sucks blood from me.

Kirsten does a swift crawl stroke over to my

rock. "You're not going to sit there all night, are you? Come on in and have some fun."

"I'm not really in the mood. . . . "

"Oh, *please*." Kirsten rolls her eyes. "I hope you're not going to act this way when we're on the road."

For a second, it feels as though the wind has been knocked right out of me. "I'm not going with you, remember? I told you I'm going to school in the fall."

"That's right . . . " Kirsten nods. "For a minute there, I totally forgot you decided to give up your dream so you could do what your parents wanted instead. Thanks for reminding me."

My face is getting hot. "I'm not giving up anything. . . . "

Kirsten's tuned out by now and has set her sights on pulling me into the water. She grabs one of my ankles and gives it a firm tug. Her strength catches me off guard.

"You *don't* want to be doing that," I say, fighting her off with my other foot.

"Drag her in!" Jay shouts.

The hot dog people are looking, the boat guy is looking, even the fish are looking. My hands are losing their grip on the smooth surface of the rock. With a few more tugs, I've lost the battle and I feel myself sliding down the front of the rock into the cool water below.

And when I come up, I'm laughing.

Hey, Val! How've you been?"

Jay looks up from his newspaper and stares at the phone receiver in my hand. His eyes look like they could pop right out of his head.

"Miserable," Val says thickly. "How's Jay?"

"Uh, well, you know how it is—he's hanging in there . . . ," I say.

Jay violently shakes his head and waves his arms wildly, mouthing the words, *I'm not here. I don't want to talk to her.*

Val sniffles. "Can I talk to him?"

I shoot Jay a questioning look, but he still refuses. Sighing, I roll my eyes to the ceiling and give him an annoyed frown. The only thing worse than being in the middle of this mess is having to lie about it, too.

"He can't come to the phone right now—he's sort of busy," I say.

Val is silent for a moment. "You mean he doesn't want to talk to me, right?"

I clench my teeth. "Yeah."

She exhales into the receiver. "I returned the dress, you know, and sent all my bridal magazines to the recycling center. I know I went overboard, but I'm all done with that now. I just want him back."

Jay is still staring at me, so I turn around and face the wall. As far as I'm concerned, by not talking to her, he's surrendered all rights to the conversation.

"I know you do," I answer soothingly. I wish there was something more I could say to make her feel better. "You might have to give it some time."

"You have to admit, though, that I wasn't the only one who overreacted," she says. "If I had known he was going to flip out like that, I never would've—"

"I know." A wave of guilt washes over me. "I was surprised, too."

"It's crazy to throw everything away on a simple misunderstanding. . . . "

"You're totally right."

"Do you think he knows that?" she chokes. "Do you think he knows how much I miss him?"

Stealing a sly peek over my shoulder, I see Jay craning his neck and squinting, obviously trying hard to listen in. "I can't answer that," I whisper into the phone.

"Can you at least tell him I'm sorry?"

My heart feels heavy for her. "Of course I will, Val. We'll talk again, okay?"

"Okay. Thanks."

"Take care, all right?"

When I hang up, Jay practically pounces on me for info. "What did she say?" he asks.

I take a seat at the table. "If you want to know, you'll have to call her yourself."

Jay leans forward until he's practically in my face. "Come on, M."

"Val returned the dress. She feels really bad about everything," I say as a gnawing sensation spreads throughout my stomach. It's time to come clean. "Besides, if there's anyone you should be mad at, it's me—not her."

"Huh?"

"Well . . . " My throat tightens in a painful spasm, cutting off my breath. "Val didn't pull the whole marriage idea out of the air. She got it from me."

Jay regards me with a long, silent stare that makes me shiver. "Keep going . . . "

"It was the day we went to the park," I squeak. "She was feeling really down—she thought you didn't love her anymore because you were acting distant."

"I just love the idea of my sister and my girl-friend psychoanalyzing my every move," he says crossly, rolling his eyes. "So what did *you* say?"

I chew nervously on my lower lip. "I said that you were probably just overtired and that I was sure you loved her and that I was sure you were going to marry her someday." I pause for a second to catch my breath. This is *so* hard. "I told her I thought you were saving up to buy her a ring."

Jay's eyes go cold. "Why did you say that?"

"Because I thought it was true! Remember when we were in the restaurant and I asked you—"

"And I told you flat out I wasn't ready."

Groaning, I let my arms flop on the table and I rest my head. "I thought you were just saying that so I'd stop bugging you."

The tips of his ears redden. "Even if I was, you still had no business saying that to Val," he says.

"I know." Stinging tears of embarrassment well up in the corners of my eyes. "I'm *so* sorry, Jay. I know it was a stupid thing to do, but I didn't mean any harm. If you'd been there, you would've seen how innocently it all happened."

With a tired exhale, Jay gives my wrist a forgiving pat. "Actually, this whole thing has less to do with you than you might think. I didn't break it off with Val just because of what happened at her parents' house—I'd been thinking about it even before you got here."

I brush a lock of damp hair out of my face. "What happened?"

"It wasn't any one thing, exactly," he says somberly. "It had more to do with seeing Val in a different light, I guess. Like I told you—she hasn't seemed like the same person to me now that she's on her home turf. Everything she does is linked someway to her parents. If she's not bending over backwards to make her mom happy, she's doing something rebellious to make her father mad."

"People act differently around their parents," I say. "It doesn't mean that's who she really is. Wait until you go back to school. Things will get better."

Jay traces invisible patterns on the kitchen table with his finger. "Maybe *this* is how she really is, and *school* makes her act differently. I've started thinking that maybe Val was just going out with me to tick her dad off—you know, she's the one who suggested I volunteer for Habitat. She knew it would really make him furious."

"That is *so* wrong, Jay," I say. "Val doesn't operate like that, and you know it. She loves you, and I'm not just guessing this time. You should talk to her—I know you guys can patch things up."

Staring down at his hands, Jay's chest rises and falls heavily as if a giant weight is pressing down on him. "At this point, M," he says darkly, "I'm not even sure I want to."

After a tiring week of finishing most of the exterior of Leann's house, the three of us decide to take a road trip to Monticello, Thomas Jefferson's famous estate. We bring Darren along, too, because we're scared to leave him home by himself. Our little tour group arrives at the parking lot just in time to catch the first shuttle bus of the day up the small mountain. Even though it's pretty early in the morning, Jay is completely in his glory, just busting with pertinent historical facts. History doesn't sit well with me this early—it's like eating lasagna for breakfast.

"Did you know Monticello actually means 'little mountain' in Italian?" Jay says this like he thinks we really care. "Jefferson drew heavily on Italian Renaissance architecture in the design of his home. Later, during the expansion of Monticello, Jefferson incorporated French influences."

Kirsten gives me a little nudge in the ribs with her elbow, and we both start to laugh. I turn around and face Darren and Jay in the seat behind us. "I'll take 'Useless Information' for two hundred dollars, Alex," I joke.

Kirsten giggles. "Instead of taking books out of the library to do research, kids can just check Jay out for the day. He'll tell you everything you need to know!"

"And they can stick one of those stamp cards in his shirt pocket!" I laugh.

"Are you done?" Jay doesn't find it as amusing as we do, but his good mood keeps him from taking us too seriously.

Even Darren starts hee-hawing, and soon we're all laughing so hard, we're nearly crying.

"I guess you guys are walking home tonight," Jay teases, looking out the window as we wind up the hill.

As I finally catch my breath, the thought hits me that despite our differences, Kirsten and I probably would've had a great time driving cross-country. Even though she can be completely manipulative, Kirsten has this way of bringing out the lighter, more daring side in people, which would probably be good for me. On the flip side, I think that maybe I rein her in just enough to keep her from going too far sometimes. Together, I think maybe we would've struck the right balance.

"I've been thinking a lot lately about taking Route 80," Kirsten says out of the blue, as if she's read my mind. "It goes north around Chicago and then goes straight west all the way to San Francisco—I figured we could visit your friend Chloe when we get there."

"Kirsten, stop it—" I plead.

"What?" she says, all wide-eyed and innocent. "What did I say?"

I frown, my chest feeling like it's being weighted down by a sandbag. "You keep talking about the trip and I already told you, I don't think I'm going."

Kirsten gives me a sly, crooked smile. "You're still dead set on going to school, huh? I can respect that, I guess. A chance like this doesn't happen too often, though. Remember—you can go to school anytime."

"I can travel anytime, too," I argue. "It doesn't have to be right this second."

"Don't be so sure," Kirsten says, shaking her head. "I mean, you're going to be tied up with school for the next four years, right? You'll have to work during the summers, so that's out. And after college, you'll be too busy searching for a job and looking for an apartment to take some time off. Think about it. This might be your only chance."

I turn away from her and stare out the window, feeling the weight sink deeper and deeper into me until I can hardly breathe anymore. Intellectually, I know that Kirsten's just saying these things because she has her own agenda—she wants me to come along and keep her company. She doesn't really care what's best for me, and nothing that she's saying is necessarily true. Yet, on an emotional level, my insides are churning and screaming, *You know she's right . . . you should go with her. . . .*

For the rest of the trip up the mountain, I feel strangely somber, as if the joy's been sucked out of the day. But when we finally reach the top, my peaceful state of mind returns. The moment we get off the bus, each of us is struck by the breathtaking beauty of the regal mansion waiting for us at the end of the walkway, with its clean, symmetrical design and stately dome resting on top.

Darren digs a nickel out of his pocket with his good hand and holds it up in the air, squeezing one eye shut. "Looks like we're at the right place," he says, comparing the real building to its likeness on the back of the coin.

Somehow I thought the building would look kind of tired and sad—after all, Jefferson built the thing over two hundred years ago—but it's obviously been kept in immaculate condition. It makes me feel like we're in some weird time warp where we've been accidentally booted back to 1782.

I nudge Jay with my elbow. "After we have lunch with Thomas Jefferson, what do you say we borrow a couple of his horses and pay a visit to Colonel Walter Lewis? I'd like to meet the old guy."

Jay groans. "You can go without me."

We gather in the entrance of the house, along with twenty or so touristy-looking people, while a slight man in scholarly horn-rimmed glasses introduces himself as Jonathan, our tour guide. The floor is a stunning green, and the room is decorated with interesting objects such as oil paintings, antlers, black-and-gold Windsor chairs, and even a clock that shows not only seconds, minutes, and hours, but also the day of the week. Jonathan explains that this is the area of the house where guests would wait to be greeted by Jefferson— James and Dolley Madison being some of our third president's more frequent guests.

Kirsten leans toward me. "What's he doing?" she whispers in my ear.

I give her a puzzled look. "Who?"

With a twitch of her head, Kirsten discreetly nods to the corner of the room. My eyes follow to where Darren is standing in front of a painting, his fingers gently tracing the gilded edge of the frame.

"Excuse me, sir," Jonathan calls sternly to him. Everyone looks up, but Darren is totally oblivious to what's going on. "Sir, with the cast," Jonathan repeats. "We do not touch the artwork here."

"Apparently, some of us do . . . ," Jay jokes under his breath.

It takes Darren a second to figure out what's going on, then he backs away and smiles, stumbling over one of the antique chairs as he waves at our very ruffled tour guide. Pinching his lips together, Jonathan gives Darren one more stern look of warning before leading the rest of us to the next room.

Kirsten grabs my elbow and holds me back while Jay, Darren, and the rest of the group move on. "I have to ask you something," she says like she's about to hatch some top secret plot. "Is Jay seeing anyone?"

Startled, I pull away from her. "Why do you want to know?"

"Don't get all huffy," she answers coolly. "I was just curious. A guy like Jay's got to have a hottie or two stashed away somewhere."

I laugh uneasily. "I'm not exactly sure where things stand right now, but he's been seeing a woman named Val for almost two years. They had this little fight the day you arrived—a misunder-standing, actually—but they've been kind of slow to patch things up. But they're really a great cou-ple—I know it'll all work out."

"But they're not technically together," Kirsten clarifies.

Warning sirens go off in my head. "Yes—I mean no . . . ," I stammer. "Don't even think about it, Kirsten. I mean it. My brother's off limits."

Kirsten furrows her brow, looking offended. "Jeez, don't sweat it. Like I said, I was just curious."

It's hard not to be impressed by all the interesting innovations scattered throughout Jefferson's house, many of which seem almost modern. One of my favorites is the alcove beds, which were nestled between walls to save space. Jefferson's own bed was placed in what looks like a large doorway between rooms—so that when he rolled out of one side of the bed, he could be in his study, and when he rolled out of the other side of his bed, he could be in his bedroom. In the parlor are two doors that are rigged so that when one is opened or closed, the other door also opens or closes, seemingly by itself. The study has a rotating reader's stand that holds five books at once and a fascinating little machine Jefferson purchased called a polygraph. It's a simple device comprised of two pens connected together so that what ever the user wrote with one pen was automatically copied by the second. Kind of like a primitive photocopier.

As cool as the house is, my enthusiasm for Jefferson wanes when Jonathan mentions that most of the estate's upkeep was handled by the 150 slaves Jefferson kept on Mulberry Row, a road near the house. The slaves worked as blacksmiths, carpenters, dairy farmers, launderers, and gardeners, all to maintain the estate. Even though he owned slaves, some historians say that Jefferson was against slavery—which, if you ask me, doesn't make a whole lot of sense. They say that while he thought slavery was fundamentally wrong, he believed it to be too big a problem to be solved during his lifetime. It makes me sad to think that this brilliant man didn't use his power and influence to put an end to the horror of slavery once and for all. I mean, some things are too important to just sit back and wait for someone else to fix. Sometimes, you just have to take care of it yourself.

When the tour is over, we check out the dependencies, which are areas in the basement where the kitchen, wine cellar, and icehouse are located. Compared to the clean, cheeriness of the house, the dependencies are dark and dank, smelling of rich soil and cold stone.

"This is cool," Darren murmurs, wandering behind me through the dark passageway. I turn around to make sure we're not moving too fast for Jay, the incurable history buff, but when I look back, he's nowhere in sight.

"Where's Jay?" I ask. "Did we lose him in the wine cellar?"

Darren shrugs. "I haven't seen him since the

tour was over. Come to think of it, I haven't seen Kirsten, either."

I scan the group of people ahead of us in the kitchen, but Jay and Kirsten aren't there. "Maybe they didn't know we went down here. We should find them—they're probably looking for us."

Darren and I head back through the dark passage into the daylight, expecting Jay and Kirsten to be searching frantically for us near the entrance, but they're not there, either. "I bet Jay's still poking around the house," Darren says. "He probably hasn't even realized the tour's over."

"Kirsten would notice." We walk up to the front door of the house to see if Jay's still inside. Luckily, our tour guide, Jonathan, is in the main entrance ready to start his next group. "Excuse me," I say to the man. "I'm looking for my brother. He was in your last tour—is there a chance he's still inside?"

Jonathan glares at Darren from behind his scholarly glasses, obviously remembering the unfortunate incident with the painting. "There is no one left. Perhaps he is touring the grounds."

"This is weird," I say as we go back outside and head toward the West Lawn. "It's not like Jay to just go off like that. Kirsten, I can see—but not Jay."

"Maybe they didn't have a choice," Darren says in an eerie voice. "Maybe they were abducted by aliens."

I laugh. "How dare they go into outer space without us!"

"Hey—" Darren stops suddenly. "Is that them, over there?"

My eyes follow Darren's pointing finger to a bench not far from the fishpond. "Yeah, it looks like them," I say, recognizing the unmistakable wave of my brother's reddish-brown hair. "Looks like the aliens brought them back in one piece."

"Maybe they brought us some souvenirs," Darren jokes. Instead of going over to the bench to let Jay and Kirsten know we're still alive, both Darren and I are frozen still in our tracks. There's a definite "do not disturb" vibe coming from their direction that we're picking up on. Maybe it's because it looks like they're deep in conversation. Or maybe it's because they're sitting so close together, you'd think they shared a pair of lungs and maybe a kidney or two.

"Should we bother them?" Darren says, looking uncomfortable.

As if to answer his question, Kirsten tilts her head up toward my brother and gently touches the side of his face with her fingertips. In less than ten seconds, she's got him in a lip-lock that would take the Jaws of Life to pry loose.

"I guess not," I answer, looking away.

I'm so completely annoyed right now, I could just scream.

Kirsten and Jay spend the better part of an hour hanging all over each other while Darren and I poke around the gardens making small talk to cover up our embarrassment. It ticks me off that Kirsten went right in for the kill right after I told her Jay was involved with someone else. Does the girl have no shame? He's my brother! You don't just make a move on your friend's brother like that, especially when you plan on tossing him away like a candy bar wrapper. And Jay's no better—you don't scoop your sister's friend even if she *is* flirty and gorgeous and is staying in your apartment for a while. Does he honestly believe Kirsten would be a better girlfriend than Val ever was?

Are they insane? Why am I the only person who's making any sense?

When Jay and Kirsten are done inspecting each other's tonsils, they finally come looking for us.

"Does anyone need to go to the . . . um . . . ?"

Jay's face goes blank for a second. "You know, the whatchamacallit?"

"You mean *the bathroom?*" I snap.

"Yeah!" he says, his eyes lighting up. "Does anyone need to go to the bathroom before we hit the road?"

Kirsten must be some kisser, I think wryly to myself. *She sucked Jay's brain right out of his head like a vacuum cleaner. Nice job, Hoover.*

"I'm fine," Kirsten says with a self-satisfied smirk.

"Me, too," I say, crossing my arms in front of me. "I'm just fine."

"Okay," Jay says, flashing a dopey grin. "I'll be right back then." He turns around a couple of times like a dog chasing his tail, then heads down toward the garden.

I roll my eyes. "Hey, Knucklehead—the bathrooms are this way," I say, pointing in the opposite direction. A short burst of Darren's laughter explodes in my ears. "Would you go with my brother so he doesn't get lost?" I ask him.

"I'm all right," Jay protests, turning himself around to face in the right direction. "I'm just feeling a little light-headed because my blood sugar is dropping." Jay starts to head off on his own, but a heavy glance from me sends Darren running after him.

I know Kirsten and I are only going to be alone for a few minutes, so I get right to the point. "I saw you guys making out on the bench," I say, the muscles in my face tightening into a scowl. "I guess all that history makes you crazy, huh?"

"I wasn't crazy at all," Kirsten says, still smirking.

"It seems to me you'd have to be crazy to make a move on a guy who has a girlfriend," I say, my voice dripping with sarcasm. "Or is that part of the attraction?"

Kirsten gives me one of those blank you've-got-to-be-kidding-me looks, then says something that makes me shudder. "You're so uptight, Miranda."

"And you're careless with people's feelings," I counter, still reeling from the sting of her remark. "You have a habit of making promises and not following through with them."

The words peel away Kirsten's carefree attitude like a mask. "I knew you'd bring that up again."

"I don't have a lot to go on," I say firmly. "I don't want to see you trashing my brother like you trashed me."

Kirsten falls silent, her eyes downcast. "There's so much more going on here than you know," she says a moment later. "You should really keep your opinions to yourself until you know what you're talking about."

"So why don't you fill me in?" I ask, holding my ground. "Tell me everything—I'm dying to hear it."

"I really don't feel like going into it with you," Kirsten says decidedly. "If you really want to know, then you're going to have to ask your brother."

Later that night, I'm standing outside Jay's room, trying to decide if I should go in. After having had a little time to cool down, the thought crossed my mind that maybe the whole Val-Jay-Kirsten love triangle was really none of my business at all and I should give it a rest. Still, there's this nagging feeling in my gut that's pushing me along, keeping me involved. We *are* talking about my only brother's happiness and well-being here—what's his business is mine, too.

I knock.

"Come in." Jay is stretched out on his bed, his nose buried in yet another thick economics book. "Hey, M."

"Are you busy?"

"Not really," he says, closing the book. "Did you have fun today?"

"Yeah, it was pretty cool." I plop down, cross-legged, beside him. "But I did see something that disturbed me quite a lot."

"Oh?"

"Yeah—when I saw you kissing Kirsten."

I lay it out so flat that Jay is completely dumbstruck for several minutes. He stares at me with bulging eyes and keeps patting his chest like he's just swallowed a fly. "I didn't know we had an audience," he chokes.

"Don't worry, we couldn't stand watching for very long."

Jay's complexion turns a light shade of pink. He looks embarrassed and irritated with me all at the same time. "So now I suppose you're going to lecture me on the evils of getting involved with Kirsten."

"Something like that," I say. "I'm not sure you know what you're getting into with her. She's not the most stable person I've ever met."

"Do you always say such nice things about your friends?" he says with a sarcastic edge. "Remind me not to get on your bad side."

"Okay, maybe that was a little harsh," I admit sheepishly. "But she's not your type, Jay—she's restless and irresponsible. Most of the time the only person she cares about is herself. Was that more diplomatic?"

"Hardly." Jay leans back against his pillow. "I thought we agreed a while ago not to tell each other how to live our lives."

I shrug innocently. "Does that mean I can't give you my opinion when I think you're making a huge mistake?"

Jay shakes his head. "It means having enough confidence in a person to trust they'll make the best choice for themselves," he says. "I've been really good about not nagging you anymore—why can't you do the same for me?"

"I'm not nagging," I insist. "I'm simply passing along information to help you make an informed decision. I'm providing a valuable service."

"Good line," he says. "I'll have to remember that one."

"Okay, so maybe I *am* nagging, but it's not such a bad thing, you know. There have been plenty of times when you've bugged me about something and later on I've realized that you were totally right."

Jay raises a skeptical eyebrow at me. "Oh, yeah? Like when?"

"Like when I started working on the house. I was totally resistant at first, even though you kept saying I'd love it, and then after a while I really *did* get into it, just like you said. Instead of fighting with you, I should've trusted your judgment because you obviously knew what you were talking about."

Rubbing his chin pensively, Jay looks caught somewhere between being proud of his powers of influence over me and confused as to where all of this is leading.

"And then there's college," I continue. "It used to drive me nuts when you kept pestering me to go to Yale, but after spending some time here, I've come to the decision that you're right about that, too—so I've decided to enroll for the fall semester."

Instead of being elated like I'd hoped, Jay's face falls. "Don't, M," he says with complete seriousness. "Don't give up on your dream."

I blink at him in stunned disbelief, a dull, piercing ache radiating through my torso as if I'd just been sucker punched. "What do you mean?"

"If you really want to go to school, that's great, but make sure you're going for the right reasons and not because you want to please me, or tick off Kirsten, or make Mom and Dad proud," he says earnestly, his hazel eyes tinged with a mysterious sadness. "I think sometimes you're a little too concerned about what other people think to make your own decisions."

Even though I don't want to believe what he's saying, the truth of Jay's words cut deeply inside me with their stinging accuracy. My mind is fuzzy and confused. One minute he's telling me to go to school, the next he's telling me not to. What am I supposed to do?

"But I don't know what I want, Jay," I say, my voice almost pleading. "That's why I listen to what other people think—I figure, the more opinions I get, the closer I'll be to finding an answer."

"It doesn't always work that way. Everyone's going to have a different idea of what you should do, but that doesn't mean they're right—I've had a taste of that myself recently," Jay says. "You're an adult now, M. You have to look to yourself for the answers."

Maybe the idea of having to rely solely on yourself is supposed to be a comforting thought, but it just makes me feel isolated and alone. I wish I could go back in time and be a kid again, when everyone told me what to do. Life was a lot easier when I didn't have any choices.

"So, you think I should go on the trip?" No sooner are the words spoken, I realize I'm doing it again—asking for everyone else's opinion except my own. "I'll make my own decision, of course," I correct. "But I'm just curious what you think."

"Okay," Jay says, smiling. "I thinking you have a strong desire to see what's out there in the world and you won't be satisfied until you do it."

"I'll take that into consideration," I say, nodding slowly. "You know, you still owe me a favor from the bet you lost."

"What do you want?" he asks ruefully. "My car? Money for a plane ticket?"

I fix him with a dead-serious stare. "I want you to stop seeing Kirsten."

Groaning, Jay covers his eyes with his hands. "You haven't heard a word I've said, have you?"

"You'll get attached, I know it—and then she'll take off, and you'll be crushed. I know her."

"I know her, too." Jay falls silent for several minutes, and when he starts to speak again, I get the strange sensation that he's about to tell me something I might not necessarily want to hear. "Remember, we were friends in high school."

"Lab partners," I correct.

"More than lab partners," Jay says heavily. "The truth is, we dated for a while."

My jaw drops, and my body goes numb with shock. *So this is what Kirsten meant when she said there was more to the story*, I think silently as my stomach turns sour. Taking my eyes off Jay, I focus on an old cobweb clinging to the white wall above his head. It's really hard to look at him right now.

"What did you do? Go out a few times to discuss your lab reports over milk shakes?" I say, laughing weakly.

"It was more intense than that," my brother whispers. "Actually, we were together for a few months."

"A few months?" my voice cracks. "How come I don't remember any of this?"

"Because we didn't tell anyone," Jay admits.

This is totally bizarre, I tell myself in silent panic. *I must've slipped into some parallel universe where everyone looks the same, but they've all gone wacko.*

While I search my brother's face to comprehend what he's telling me, his features seem to shift and change imperceptibly, turning him into someone I don't even recognize. Ultimately, it hardly matters that Jay once dated Kirsten—what's tough to take is realizing that my own brother kept an important secret from me, something he probably never planned on revealing if I hadn't forced the issue. How many more secrets is he keeping?

"So Mom and Dad didn't know?" I ask. "What about your friends?"

Jay looks down at the bed and picks tiny balls of lint off the covers. "No one knew. At the time, I don't think we were consciously trying to keep our relationship a secret, but now that I look back, I think we were afraid people would give us flack for being together. We avoided each other in school, except for chem lab, telling ourselves it was because we hung out with different groups of friends who didn't mix. It just seemed easier that way."

I can imagine the school controversy: *Jayson Burke and Kirsten Greene—hot new couple or tragic victims of chem lab fumes?* With Jay reigning as class darling and poster boy for perfection, and Kirsten's reputation as a troublemaking outsider, there's no doubt that they were an explosive combination in our small, status-conscious school.

A faint, nostalgic glow brightens Jay's face. "We used to meet on weeknights after dinner or on weekends. We never went anywhere in town, so we wouldn't be seen together. Sometimes we'd even go into New York so we could be completely anonymous."

"If it was so much trouble, why did you bother?" I ask.

For a moment, Jay seems at a loss to explain it. "It was like we were living in a world of our own—separate from everything and everyone else. We had this really strong magnetic attraction, and even though we were two entirely different people, none of it mattered when we were away from our normal day-to-day lives," he says. "I know you have your issues with Kirsten, but you have to admit that when she's around, you never know what's going to happen next. She made me want to take chances, to try new things—she made me realize that even though I'd been conservative and predictable my whole life, I didn't have to be trapped by it. I could be any person I wanted to be."

Jay might as well be taking these words straight from my own head, because that's how Kirsten made me feel, too. I noticed a long time ago that she never pigeonholed people into categories or types and she never limited them by buying into the roles we were all forced to play. Kirsten never saw people for who they were—she saw them for who they could be.

"So what happened?" I ask. "Were the secret meetings wearing you down?"

Jay nods. "And the fact that our differences were too big to ignore. She totally agreed. It was a perfect short-term romance, but we really didn't have a future together. After getting a glimpse of what could have been, I was happy to go back to a regular life with no secrets."

I take a minute or two to let it all soak in. "So now that you're out of school and you don't have to hide anymore, you figured you could try to pick things up again with her."

"I was really tempted. I mean the attraction's still—well, it's pretty strong," Jay answers slowly. "But I didn't think it could really go anywhere—especially with Kirsten leaving. She told me she'd stay if I wanted her to, but the more I thought about it, the more I started to miss Valerie."

"You mean you want to get back with her?" I ask, my heart surging with hope.

Jay nods. "I'd like to try—if she'll have me. These last few days without her have made me realize just how much she means to me."

"That's so great, Jay!" I throw my arms around him and give him a huge hug. "I'm so glad you're giving it another chance—Val's worth it."

He smiles shyly. "I think so, too."

As we enter the final phase of the building project, our crew gets bigger every day. Volunteers from local universities and churches, as well as Habitat families from all over the county, are pitching in to help us with the millions of details we still have left to do. Doors still need to be hung, exterior trim has to be painted, plus the landscaping needs to be planned for the property. On the inside there's still a lot of painting to do, carpet and vinyl flooring to be laid, sinks and toilets and kitchen cabinets to put in. Gary's divided the volunteers into shifts working almost around the clock to make sure we finish the job on time. The mood is still light, but there's an underlying intensity present as we deal with all the frustrating little problems that keep cropping up—like the refrigerator being delivered late and the store that was supposed to donate the bathroom fixtures backing out at the last minute. Even with all the craziness, it's still amazing to stand back and watch a bunch of virtual strangers coming together to help someone in need.

Finally, the big day arrives—one day ahead of schedule, no less. Gary recruited some of his friends to work through the night, and when we arrive at the site the next morning, there's nothing left to do but clean up. Leann is supposed to come by to work at around lunchtime, so we scramble to vacuum the carpets and wash the windows before she gets here. The whole crew is frantic and excited, like we're planning a surprise party. Kirsten and I go to the local florist and buy a pretty grapevine wreath with dried flowers to hang on the front door. Jay and Darren get a big, round, decorated cake with WELCOME HOME LEANN AND NOAH on it written in fancy script. After Marcy hangs an enormous red ribbon across the doorway of the front porch, we all stand around, waiting in restless anticipation for Leann to arrive.

"I think I see her car," someone calls out. After the sighting has been confirmed, we line up in front of the house like fidgety little kids posing for a class picture. I stand in the front row so I can see the look of surprise on Leann's face, my spine tingling as her rusty old car makes its seemingly endless trip to the end of the road. A few laughs ripple through the crowd as the car stops in front of the house. We're all beaming.

"What's going on here?" Leann asks, her eyes darting from one grinning face to the next. She gets Noah out of his car seat and walks up the new cement path, looking slightly confused. "Is something wrong? Are we going to have to wait a few more weeks?"

The crowd parts down the middle, and we all step aside so Leann can get a better look. The one-story house is small but pristine with its clean wood shingles and crisp white trim. The newly planted bushes stand perfectly against the front of the house. A wooden porch swing that was donated by the lumber company hangs in stillness just waiting to be used, right next to the thick woven welcome mat that's never been stepped on. If you ask any one of us right now, I think we'll all tell you that this is probably one of the proudest moments of our lives.

Leann stares at the big red ribbon, her mouth trembling.

Gary steps forward, his face flush with emotion. "Leann, here are the keys to your new house," he says, while we all burst into cheers and applause. Tears spring to my eyes so fast, I hardly have a chance to catch them without being seen, but as I look around, it's clear I'm not the only one who's moved.

"I can't believe this," Leann gasps, accepting her keys. She clasps her hands to her mouth and starts to cry. "I swear this is the most beautiful house I've ever seen. Thank you all so much—"

When she stops shaking, Leann is handed a

pair of scissors and cuts the ribbon in two while we cheer wildly. People swarm Leann to offer their congratulations and lead her inside to show her the finished interior. Kirsten and I hang back and wait for the crowd to ease up.

"I'm glad they can finally move in, but I'm a little sad the whole thing is over," I confess, taking a seat on the front steps. "I kind of felt like it was my house, too."

"You could always stick around and build another one if you wanted," Kirsten says.

"Nah," I say, shaking my head. "I've decided to do a little traveling instead."

Lazily, Kirsten stretches her legs out in front of her. "Not going to school, huh?"

I shrug. "I don't know—maybe I'll just poke around for the summer and go to school in the fall. I haven't really decided yet. Right now, all I'm thinking about is heading for the West Coast."

"Sounds cool." Kirsten sighs. "Mind if I tag along?"

"Well . . . ," I say hesitantly.

"I have a car," she adds.

"And a full tank of gas?"

Kirsten nods. "And a box of granola bars in the trunk."

"In that case, you're in," I say with a laugh.

After what happened in Cape May, I never dreamed I'd give Kirsten another chance, but here we are, trying for a second time to get our big trip off the ground. Some people might call me a sucker for trusting her again, but they're way off base, because things are truly different this time. It's not that I believe Kirsten has suddenly become more reliable; it's that I've learned not to expect so much from her. In New York I sat back, thinking she would take care of me and look out for me the whole time, and when that didn't happen, I was crushed. But I'll never be disappointed again. Kirsten might get flighty and weird and maybe she'll even ditch me in the middle of Iowa without warning—and it won't matter. She can do whatever she wants. I know what I'm dealing with this time.

"There's been a question on my mind for the last several days that I was hoping you could answer," I say. "When you talked to me in study hall, was it because you wanted to be friends or was it because you were prying me for information about my brother?"

Kirsten grins. "Well, at first, of course, it was because of Jay," she says unapologetically. "But I thought you were an okay kid, too."

"Gee, thanks," I say, rolling my eyes.

"No, seriously—when I started to get to know you, I really liked you," she says.

Staring down at my hands, I work at a stubborn hangnail, feeling a little bit like a chump. I've always prided myself on my ability to read people, to sniff out insincerity and manipulation with the accuracy of a search dog. More and more I'm starting to think that maybe I can't trust my instincts about people at all.

"I know you see me as some sort of professional flirt who devours guys like popcorn, but it's not true." Kirsten stares ahead, her eyes seeming to focus on the approaching line of white clouds just now making an appearance above the tree line. "Remember when we went to the movies in Cape May and you asked me if I'd ever been in love?"

I nod slowly, remembering the conversation clearly. "You said you met some guy on a camping trip when you were fifteen."

"And I also said I fell in love when I was seventeen, with a guy at school," she says, her eyes distant. "I was talking about Jay."

An electric bolt seizes my spine, leaving me too stunned to talk. Why am I so surprised? Disregarded bits of memory come together with new meaning—the look on Kirsten's face in New York when she asked about Jay; the way she pounced on him in the driveway and at Monticello; her refusal to even let me guess who the mystery man was that she had fallen so madly in love with. Why didn't I see it?

Kirsten swallows hard, her face softened by the reopening of an old wound. "I was devastated when he broke it off with me, but I knew he was right. It couldn't have lasted. When I came here and saw him again, I'll admit a small part of me was hoping he'd change his mind. At the very least, I wanted to show him what he was missing."

I reach out and put my arm around Kirsten, wondering if Jay ever knew how much she had fallen for him. "Were you okay when he told you he wanted to stay with Valerie?"

"It's never fun to be rejected," she admits. "But I wasn't as crushed as last time. Besides, there's a country full of guys to meet—statistically, there's bound to be a few good ones in the bunch."

My eyes narrow. "Hey! You'd better save one or two for me. . . . "

The screen door slaps, startling us both so much that we nearly jump out of our respective skins. When we look back, Darren is standing over us, wielding a rather large kitchen knife coated with frosting. He's holding the thing in his fist, blade pointing down, like a zombie in a slasher movie.

"Sorry to bother you guys," he says, looking at us with a look of total helplessness. "But do either one of you know anything about cutting cakes?"

So you're happy with it?" I ask Leann for the umpteenth time, in between bites of mutilated cake. It's a stupid question, but I love to see the look of total bliss that comes over her face every time I ask. "You really like it?"

Leann's damp eyes glaze over, and her voice swells with emotion. "I just couldn't be happier. I'm staying here tonight—I don't even care that I don't have a bed yet. I'm sleeping on the floor."

Noah pushes a plastic dump truck across the smooth brown-and-beige kitchen floor, weaving in and out of the forest of adult ankles and feet. I wonder if he realizes yet that this is his new home.

"So are you going to stick around for a while?" Leann asks, graciously pushing aside her own glory for the moment to find out what's happening with me. "Or have you decided to keep moving on?"

"I'm leaving tomorrow," I say, my voice still a bit hesitant. "Kirsten and I are going to hit the road and see where we end up."

Leann gives me a happy hug. "That sounds wonderful. Have a great time."

"I'm definitely going to try," I say with a nervous smile. "It's kind of scary not knowing what lies ahead."

"Tell me about it," Leann answers. "But life never throws you more than you can handle. When things get tough, think of it as an opportunity to see your own strength. And then, lots of times, things turn out better than you ever could've imagined." She turns around absentmindedly and opens the refrigerator, as if in all of her excitement she forgot to look at it earlier. "This sure beats the dinosaur in my old apartment. Too bad you won't be around to see the place once I get some furniture. If you ever pass through this way again, we'd love to have you stop in for a visit. We could have dinner, and you could tell me all about your life on the road."

I smile. "I'll bring the peanut butter."

Dear Mom, Dad, and Abby!

I've just finished packing, and Kirsten is at the gas station filling up the tank. As soon as she gets back, we're hitting the road. I can't wait to get moving! Jay seems heartbroken that we're leaving—he can't stop talking about how his life won't be the same now that he no longer has to fight for the remote control.

I'll send you another postcard once we're west of the Mississippi.

Love and kisses to everybody,
Miranda

A car horn blares from the driveway.

"Hold on!" I shout, strapping my pack to my back as I head for the back door. Ugh! I'd forgotten how heavy the stupid thing is. It's a good thing we're not hiking across America—I'd probably be sprawled out facedown before I even got to the end of the driveway.

Jay and Darren are standing by the car, and

Kirsten sticks her tongue out at me as I come flying through the door, propelled by the momentum of my pack.

"Hurry up!" she yells at me, laying on the horn one more time for good measure.

"What are we in such a hurry for?" I thrust the postcard under Jay's nose. "Will you mail this for me?"

"Sure," he says, flipping it over.

"Don't read it!" I scold. "It's confidential!"

Jay frowns. "It's got my name on it," he says, reading my note. "I have a right to look at it."

"And please say bye to Val for me. Tell her I'm sorry I didn't get a chance to call her before I left."

"I will."

Feeling a slight tug on my pack, I spin around to see Darren standing there, his arms open. "Thanks for everything, Miranda," he says, clobbering me with an awkward hug. "I hope you have a nice trip."

Even though he's about as gentle as a grizzly bear, Darren's hug feels, well . . . *nice.*

"Thanks," I say, letting go. "When are you getting the cast off?"

"Next week."

"Good," I answer, nodding. "Make sure you go out there and get yourself a helmet for skating."

Darren wrinkles his nose. "Actually I think I'm going to sell my skates. I want to save up for a motorcycle."

I'm glad I won't be around to see that one. . . .

I give Jay a playful punch in the shoulder. "You know, brother dear, you still owe me a favor."

"Be nice . . . ," Jay groans.

An unexpected surge of emotion rises to my throat. "Will you wish me good luck?"

Jay gives me a big hug. "Of course, M. I always wish the best for you."

"Thanks for letting me stay with you and everything."

"Anytime," he says, pulling away. "Although maybe not for quite so long next time."

I give Jay a rotten look, but he just laughs and sticks his head in the driver's side window. "Kirsten—you take care of my little sister, you hear?" he says. "If she gives you any trouble, just leave her off at the nearest truck stop."

"Are you kidding? Who's going to push the car when I run out of gas?" Kirsten deadpans.

I throw my pack in the back seat. "You guys are horrible to me!"

Jay steps back as Kirsten guns the engine. "Aw, come on—you know it's just because we love you."

Before things get any sappier, Kirsten steps on the gas, and we hightail it out of there. I turn around and through the back window watch Darren and Jay waving at us before going back into the house. Darren trips as he goes up the stairs.